Critical Acclaim for Michael Farris Smith

Praise for NICK

'Gripping… NICK rings fiercely true' – *Financial Times*

'Vividly imagined and suffused with pulsing narrative energy'
– *Irish Times*

'Vivid, visual, strong, poetic' – *Herald*

'Evocative, rich in detail and memorable. You can't help but think
of *Gatsby* when reading Smith's sensitively written tale… A book
to read and reread' – *Belfast Telegraph*

'Atmospheric, haunting, rich in detail and incident'
– *Literary Review*

'Anybody who believes that the war is over when the enemy
surrenders and the troops come home needs to read Michael
Farris Smith's masterful new novel NICK. Its stark, unvarnished
truth will haunt you' – **Richard Russo**

'NICK is an exemplary novel. Smith delivers a moving, full-
bodied depiction of a man who has been knocked loose from his
moorings and is trying to claw back into his own life'
– *New York Times*

Praise for *Blackwood*

'Smith is emerging as one of the great chroniclers of America's
dispossessed' – *Mail on Sunday*

'If you're a fan of Southern or Rural Noir – James Lee Burke,
Daniel Woodrell, Donald Ray Pollock, the literary children of
Flannery O'Connor – you'll feel uncomfortably at home' – *Times*

'Outstanding' – *Strong Words*

'*Blackwood* is a fine and captivating novel with a sturdy Faulknerian theme – past and present are never exactly separated, and actions in the present are provoked by words or deeds from long ago. Michael Farris Smith's prose is calm yet full of feeling for this place and these people, and he handles scenes of introspection and scenes of hostility with equal skill. In Smith's hands, pages keep turning' – **Daniel Woodrell**

'Miraculously beautiful... Smith's prose is both raw and poetic, like opera sung at a honky-tonk. His books are tinged with reverence, an intangible and nearly religious grace that watches over the often brutal events he describes, hinting at the possibility for redemption even in the most debased' – *Los Angeles Review of Books*

'Unsettling, heartbreaking, and frequently astonishing, this Southern gothic never runs out of revelations... A gleaming, dark masterpiece by one of Southern fiction's leading voices' – *Kirkus* (starred review)

Praise for *The Fighter*

'Like living language, literary modes have both a formal and a demotic form. What we call "noir" is high tragedy brought down to the forgotten and disavowed – the fallen, who can do little but go on falling. Ours to witness the beauty and power of their fall. With *The Fighter*, cleaving to tradition, Michael Farris Smith brings that tradition brilliantly into the present' – **James Sallis**

'Smith's fiction is full of hard people in tough situations, but his obvious love of language and innately rhythmic prose lift his stories to a higher level' –*Big Issue*

'A novel that takes hold of your heart in a tight vice... *The Fighter* is also written with diamond-like care and has a visceral impact, although not always for the faint-hearted' – *Crime Time*

'Equal parts brutal and beautiful and harrowing, it's left me totally bereft' – **Chris Whitaker**

'Michael Farris Smith is continuing the southern gothic tradition of William Gay and Flannery O'Connor. Drenched in sorrow and written with complex language, *The Fighter* moves toward a conclusion both surprising and inevitable' – **Chris Offutt**

'One of those wonderful and rare books that's both a page turner and a novel of great depth and emotion. *The Fighter* is Southern Noir at its finest' – **Ace Atkins**

'Smith's great talent here is writing about ancient, universal concerns – parents and children, aging, and place – in a setting so vivid and specific that the book practically tracks mud up onto your doorstep. His vision of the Delta is powerful and lingering' – *New York Journal of Books*

Praise for *Desperation Road*

'You will not be disappointed' – *Daily Mail*

'A wonderfully evoked and deeply touching work' – *Big Issue*

'Michael Farris Smith's prose focuses on small details and has a rhythm that gives it a poetic quality; a comparison with Annie Proulx is not overly enthusiastic' – *Crime Review*

'A brilliantly compelling novel' – **Robert Olen Butler**

'A harsh but beautiful thriller that has you cheering under your breath for its wounded, fallible protagonist throughout' – *LoveReading*

'This is just stunning… little short of perfection… think Daniel Woodrell, Bill Beverly and Lou Berney for starters and that will give you an idea of the style, the range and the humanity of the novel' – **Graham Minett**

'Smith handles agony with a devastating tenderness… in a selfish, predatory world, *Desperation Road* carves out a bloody chunk of redemption' – *Crime Scene*

Also by Michael Farris Smith

The Hands of Strangers
Rivers
Desperation Road
The Fighter
Blackwood
NICK

SALVAGE

THIS

WORLD

MICHAEL FARRIS SMITH

NO EXIT PRESS

First published in the UK in 2023
by No Exit Press,
an imprint of Bedford Square Publishers Ltd.,
London, UK
noexit.co.uk
@noexitpress

A CIP catalogue record for this book is available from the British Library.

ISBN
978-0-85730-556-5 (Paperback)
978-0-85730-557-2 (eBook)

2 4 6 8 10 9 7 5 3 1

Typeset in 11.4 on 14.2pt Garamond MT Pro
by Avocet Typeset, Bideford, Devon, EX39 2BP
Printed and bound in Great Britain by Clays Ltd, Elcograf S.p.A.

MIX
Paper from
responsible sources
FSC
www.fsc.org   FSC® C018072

Sign up for our newsletter: noexit.co.uk/newsletter

For my daughters

I

1

SHE STOOD BATHED IN TWILIGHT, the dust in her hair and a kid on her hip and she stared at the approaching storm as if trying to figure how to wrangle the thunderheads and steer them to a distant and parched land where desperate souls would pay whatever ransom she demanded. The acres of sugar cane cut to nubs surrounding the house. A dry autumn turned into an unpredictable winter and then eleven days ago he left and she'd seen no one since. It was a mile walk along a dirt road that separated the acreage and another eight miles to walk to the nearest telephone but even if she wanted to bundle up and make it she wouldn't know who to call. He was gone. And he had taken the car and the cigarettes and every dollar except for the stash she kept hidden beneath a floor plank in the closet. She had finished the last of the whiskey three nights before. The milk had run out yesterday.

Jessie stared at the storm and the wind began to blow and dustclouds rose like souls awakened and she listened to the wind and welcomed the sound of something else. She shifted the child from one hip to the other and pointed out at the lightning and said look at the light. See the light? One side of the sky was thick with stormclouds and the other side of the sky was wrapped in a rustred belt that bled into the horizon like an open wound and the child lifted his small hand and pointed at the light but it was not the lightning he saw but a gathering of headlights approaching in the distance. The thunder roared and the engines roared and she turned and ran for the house, setting the child down on the porch and hurrying for the bedroom, her footfalls hard against the floorboards and her breath in quick sucks as she took the pistol from beneath the mattress and grabbed the set of keys from the dresser drawer that he had always told her to grab if she had to make a run for it and then she hustled out and scooped up the child. The headlights growing closer and splitting the dusk as she hurried around the house and along the beaten trail through the high grass that led into the woods. She ran and the child bounced in her arms and she had just reached the edge of the woods when she looked back to see the vehicles skid to a stop in front of the house, a pale and powdery cloud rising around them. She heard the engines cut and the doors slam behind her and then she heard the shouts coming in her direction as the last of twilight seeped into the earth.

They called out as they chased her into the woods and the child squeezed her neck and held on but did not cry as she ran. She had gone far into these woods before but never far enough to know if there was anything on the other side and she was seized by the thought that she may run over the edge of the earth and that she and the child would plummet soundlessly into nothing. That thought was interrupted when a shotgun fired into the night, its echo ringing through the trees. She pushed harder. Squeezing the child close to her chest. Praying not to run over the edge or if there was such a thing praying that her fall would be brief and painless. Another shotgun blast. And then another. She knew then they were looking for him. She knew there was a fine damn reason he had never returned. She knew she and the child could never go back to the house. And she knew she would have to keep running.

2

THEY SHIVERED THROUGH THE NIGHT. Jessie unbuttoned her flannel shirt and held Jace against her skin and wrapped the shirt around them both but it did not stop the shaking. He cried some. Little whimpers of discomfort. Little whimpers of hunger. She sat on a pile of leaves with her back against a white oak and held him tight. Rocked a little. Hummed and sometimes sang and she kept promising that everything was going to be all right. The boy slept in increments, the ragged sleep of distress and discomfort. An owl hooted. Nightbirds sang. Deer moved in the dark and their creeping sounded like monsters in wait.

She nodded in and out of sleep. When her eyes fell heavy she imagined strong arms and strong hands reaching for her through the dark, prying the child from her grasp and she would wake with a jerk to find herself squeezing the child so tightly he was struggling for freedom. She would stroke the back of his head and coax him back to sleep and her eyes stayed opened wide, watching the woods and watching for the arms and hands that approached in her dreams but then closing them again.

Finally there was light. She rubbed her eyes. Felt the warmth of the child's skin against her own. She did not want to wake him so she sat there and watched the morning come.

Listened to the chirps and whistles and the movement of the early creatures. The child lifted his head and coughed. Opened his eyes and looked with question at his mother.

She kissed the boy on top of his head and said it's all right. It's all right. She then tucked the empty pistol into the back of her pants and she started them walking south, believing if she kept walking south they would run into Delcambre. Amidst the trees she would stop and listen for the hum of a highway. Set the boy down and rest a minute. Listen. Then he would cry to be carried again and she would tell him to hold on. Hush a second. But he was not concerned and he cried harder and made little mad fists and she would pick him up and start again.

In an hour she came to a clearing and the earth grew soft and heavy. The damp ground sucked at her feet and she set the child down and retied the laces on her boots. He wobbled and plopped down on his behind, a smack as his ass hit the wet ground. He screamed. Something different now from toddler whimpers. He screamed and shook and slapped at his own legs, redfaced and releasing as much anger as his little body could muster. And she propped her hands on her hips and looked down at him and said let it out. Let it all out, boy.

When he was done she reached down and helped him to his feet. The back of his pants muddy. He stood next to her and they both looked out across the marshland. Cranes stood on stumps. A flock of blackbirds rose from a cluster of young cypress and scattered across the low sky. The sun sat on the horizon and lathered the marsh in gold. It seemed beautiful to her in a way she had not expected.

But there was no time to admire. The child was now wet. And hungry and cold. She was hungry and cold. She didn't know where they were but she knew there was a highway somewhere.

3

THEY CIRCLED AROUND THE EDGE of the marsh for at least an hour. Crossed into another wood where the trees thinned. The sun rose higher into a blue and cloudless sky. Their pace had slowed and the child slept with his head on his mother's shoulder. The pistol was cold and hard against the small of her back and every now and then she touched the pocket of her jeans, feeling the keys and making sure she had grabbed them and it was not part of some hurried dream.

First she saw the smoke and she followed it until she was close enough to smell it. She came to the edge of the woods and stopped. Hid herself behind a tree. Saw the small cabin with the smoke rising from its chimney and a trailer next to it. A truck sat unevenly, propped up by a jack. A front tire missing. The hood raised. Behind the truck a hatchback sat running and the driver's door was open. A cloud of exhaust from the tailpipe as the heat met the cold.

A woman stood on the cabin porch with a lit cigarette. Then another woman joined her. She held a shovel and she leaned it against the doorframe. They both wore denim jackets with collars pushed up around their necks. Both stood with their hips propped while they smoked. They talked between inhales and exhales in one and two word sentences. When they were done smoking they flicked the butts into the dirt and one of them yelled out toward the trailer. Come on. We got shit to do.

The women then stepped back inside the cabin, leaving the door open.

Jessie sprinted from the woods, the child waking with the sudden jolt and he let out a cry that she didn't acknowledge as she darted between old tires and a pile of firewood and a smoldering heap of trash and then she heard the growl as a wolf on a chain rose from slumber and lurched at her backside with its bonewhite fangs only to be held fast by a chain. She screamed and the wolf yelped but she didn't slow down, making it to the hatchback and hopping in just as a man in coveralls emerged from the trailer holding a coffee mug. He sipped and watched dumbeyed before realizing it was a stranger in the car. A stranger holding a child. He hollered and the two women came from the cabin and the three of them came down steps and ran for the hatchback as Jessie shifted into reverse, the car door open and flapping like a wing and then slamming shut when she hit the brakes, shifted into drive and stomped the gas, the tires spinning and the three of them trying to corral the hatchback like some untamed animal and as the car raced away from their cries a coffee mug crashed on the hood as if dropped from heaven, just as the tires caught firm on the gravel road.

4

S HE DROVE ALONG THE BACKROADS away from Delcambre
and toward Lake Peignur, finding a solitary gas station
where she stopped and bought a small bottle of milk and
honey buns and powdered donuts. Cigarettes and a lighter and
a pack of diapers. Then she left the store and drove east along
Highway 14, the landscape shifting from swamp to crops and
back to swamp. She turned off down a dirt road and she and
the child ate and drank until there was nothing left but to lick
the sugar from their fingertips. She changed the boy's diaper.
Leaned back the passenger seat and let him lie down while
she sat on the hood and smoked a cigarette and tried to figure
out what the hell to do.

She would need to get rid of the hatchback and she was
ready for that. The upholstery was stained and pocked with
cigarette burns and smelled sour and sick. The backseat was
piled with wadded clothes and fast food bags and as foul as
the hatchback looked and smelled she knew it had been called
in. They were not far from New Iberia and there was probably
a bus station there and she could leave the hatchback with a
nice note that said I was only borrowing it. But also in New
Iberia there would be real police made aware of the license
plate and given the description of both them and the shitty
little car.

And where the hell do you think you're taking a bus to anyway?

She made a lap around the car. Smoking and thinking. Looking in at Jace who was turned on his side and sleeping. Small hands tucked beneath his small cheek. Powdered sugar on the corners of his mouth.

She flicked away the cigarette. Looked at the heap in the backseat and it didn't matter if she was going another mile or another hundred miles she couldn't do it with this smell so she quietly opened the door. Pulled the lever on the driver's seat and it came forward and she reached into the backseat and grabbed a mess of clothes and trash. She made three trips before she had it all lying in a pile at the rear of the car and then she took the keys from the ignition and she unlocked the hatch to shove it all into the back.

But there was no room.

It was covered in garbage bags and bound with duct tape and it was big and lumpy and she knew what it was. She stepped back, tripping through the clothes and trash and falling to the ground. Up quickly and a hand over her mouth as she moved back toward the hatch and stared at it, wondering if it would jerk if she poked it. She watched carefully for any movement. Any rise and fall of breathing. Any possibility of it being something other than dead as hell. But it was still and the world held still around her as her mind could only find one thought.

Is it him?

She walked back and forth along the side of the car. Mumbling to herself. Rubbing at her face and neck. Wanting to look and to keep away. She picked up a rock and threw it and then another and another, finally crying out in disgust with not just today and yesterday but crying out against the years that had led her to now. All the steps she had taken to arrive on this empty road in the middle of nowhere with her small son asleep in a stolen car and a dead thing wrapped in a garbage bag in the hatch and she screamed out into the void and when she had screamed herself out of breath she turned and saw Jace's face in the window. Awakened by his mother. His nose and palms pressed against the glass.

She slammed the hatch before opening the car door and lifting him out. Talking to him in a flurry of motherly voice. Did you sleep okay? I didn't mean to wake you up. Do you feel better with your tummy full? Ready to ride some more?

The child shook his head at her questions. Rubbed at his eyes. Then he put his hands on her cheeks as if to hold her still and gain her full attention. Their eyes were close and the boy pushed at her cheeks.

'Home,' he said.

But I don't know where that is, she thought. I don't know which direction. I don't know what to do. And then he said it again and pressed her cheeks harder with his little hands.

'Home.'

She squeezed him. Walked down the road holding him, singing bits and pieces of songs. Fragments of lullabies and a half a verse of Amazing Grace and ending with both of them quacking like ducks. They sang and walked and she kept looking back at the hatchback as if hoping it had sunk into the earth or maybe never existed at all.

They returned to the car. Nobody would have called it in. She could drive it to the end of the world if she wanted to. But she didn't want to. She opened the milk bottle and Jace took a swallow and then she took a swallow. She settled him in the passenger seat and then she returned to the back. You have to look, she thought. You know you have to look and see if it's him.

She opened the hatch again and felt around and found the head. Pulled at the plastic bags and tore a hole and she saw matted hair and crusted blood on the forehead and she turned the face toward her and two bruised and pulpy and halfopen eyes looked at her and she gasped. Taken quickly by the stare of the dead and she stepped back and put her hands on her knees and bent over, drawing deep breaths. Settling herself. Because it was not him and she had been ready for it to be so. But she took a breath and pulled at the body and tried to wrestle it out of the hatchback. It was heavy and awkward and kept flopping back down but she finally got the legs over the side and she lifted the torso and the weight carried forward and the body tumbled out. It lay on its back. The hole in the plastic allowing its swollen eyes one last glimpse of sunlight before she turned it on its stomach and grabbed the legs and pulled it into the ditch. When she was done she turned around and Jace was standing there watching her. Holding the bottle of milk. Pointing at the thing in the ditch as if pointing at an animal in a zoo.

The wrestling and the anxiety had given her a sweat and she wiped her forehead and mouth and then she scooped up the child and began telling the story of the three little bears as she returned him to the car and buckled his seatbelt and she kept telling it as she cranked the car and as they turned back onto the highway. Jace sat silently and Jessie drove with both hands gripping the steering wheel, her forearms clenched and her shoulders clenched as she deepened her voice for papa bear and lightened it for mama bear and the rough road thumped beneath them as she told the story and tried to figure out how many years it had been since she had last spoken to her father.

5

WADE WAS LYING ON HIS back in the dreamy halfworld between sleep and consciousness, the push of the wind like some natural hypnotic as he lay there on the floor next to the fireplace where random raindrops fell down the chimney and made little taps and hisses into the remains of the fire he had kept burning through the night. Unable to sleep. The heavy gusts and the cracks of lightning that kept him awake and listening and wondering if this would be the night the house came down. He lay there and drifted back to a stormridden day of his youth, lying on the couch and watching television and listening to his mother and small sister laughing in the other room. Playing and giggling and little happy squeals echoing in his mind. One of the last days they would all be together before his mother took his sister and ran away, leaving him there with his father for reasons he both understood and never would. The winds swirled in the gray world but his memories were filled with color. Pops of yellow and green in the flowers on the shirt his sister wore. An orange ribbon tied in her hair. His mother's skyblue tanktop as she loaded the trunk of the car. The purples and blues of the bruises on her arms.

The thunder rolled and he imagined the strength of God. A feeling he had since he was a boy, drawn to a thunderstorm, watching out of his bedroom window as a storm closed in and pushed the trees and the staggered whispers through the limbs and the sway of the treetops and the winds growing stronger and stronger, his only notion of God being that of some magical creator of the heavens and the earth.

More than forty years now since he had been a boy and more than forty years now his notion of God arrived with the wind and as he lay there next to the fireplace with his back flat against the floor and his eyelids heavy and mind caught between wake and sleep he imagined the voice of God saying I created you and I can destroy you and don't you ever forget it. A bolt of lightning ripped through the sky and jerked him from his halfworld.

He sat up. He crawled across the floor and moved onto the couch, stretching out and he wiped at his face and stared at the waterstain on the ceiling. Once a tiny dot of brown that sprawled now. He rolled to his side and reached for a cigarette pack on the floor next to the couch but it was empty and he crumpled the package and tossed it into the fireplace. The rain began to weaken as he lay there. The cracks of lightning and thunderclaps lessening in volume. He knew that by the afternoon there would be a parting in the clouds and streaks of sunshine and a rich blue sky and he sighed and wished for cigarettes as he lamented that God was moving on.

Wade had dozed off again when the phone rang and woke him. It was such a rare sound that he leapt, a little jerk as his eyes opened and his head lifted from the couch cushion. I cannot think of one person, not one soul, that I want to talk to. Or that wants to talk to me. The phone kept ringing and his mind raced back across the years as he tried to imagine the face on the other end and all he could muster was the shadowed and dark.

Wade could not see her or even imagine his daughter on the other end. Pacing and mumbling to herself. Please answer. The empty parking lot of the abandoned gas station and the payphone that surprised her when she picked up the receiver and heard a dial tone. Scrounging change from the floorboards and from between the seats of the car she had stolen and hoping it was enough to make the phone dial and make the phone ring and then pausing in the middle of the number. Her eyes lost toward the horizon and the winds of loneliness blowing all around her and somewhere there was a life different from this but no notion of how to get there. She took a deep breath and squeezed her eyes shut and her thoughts were empty but for the single thing she had to do which was the same thing as the single thing she didn't want to do. Call her father. She reached down deep to find the guts. Find the courage to finish dialing and reach out to him and knowing he didn't want to hear it but what the goddamn else am I supposed to do she thought as she finished dialing the number and then swallowing hard as she waited for the call to connect. The child in her arms. The things that were chasing her. The phone ringing and for a second she wondered if he was dead. Maybe he was dead. Maybe we have come to the actual end of things. Maybe I am more alone than I imagined myself to be.

Wade lay there with his eyes closed, his irritation growing with each ring. Not even imagining that it could be her. He finally sat up. Stared at the phone on the kitchen counter and he got up. Walked over to it. Stared at it as it rang twice more and then stopped as she slammed down the receiver in the empty parking lot when the boy started to cry. He stared at the phone, relieved by its silence. Unable to imagine her walking two laps around the car and staring at the sky and wondering what could have brought her here so far away from anyone or anything. Opening the car door and putting the child down and cranking the car and thinking I will just drive. To where I don't know. I will just drive. But looking again at the phone and thinking one more time. One more time. Walking over and dropping in the coins and calling and it ringing and ringing and then he finally couldn't take it anymore so he picked up the phone.

'Daddy?' the voice said.

Something in him fell away. A great shift of the soul.

'Daddy?' she said again.

When he tried to respond he realized his breath had been sucked away and he saw her tiny foot in the palm of his rough hand and her great blue eyes of wonder and her small fingers wrapped around his thumb and if not for the faint rumble of thunder from the departing storm he would have dropped the receiver and dropped to his knees but the thunder gave him his breath and his brain and he managed to answer his daughter.

'Jessie.'

6

A LONG PAUSE. THE ANXIOUS years and the ill words and
the hard goodbyes gathering in the silence.

'Aren't you gonna say something?' she said.

'You called me.'

Another pause. He cleared this throat.

'Then you know I need something,' she said.

It's finally come, he thought. Exactly what I told her would
happen. He's run off and left her stranded or worse and it
finally has got so bad she's calling me like I said she would
one day. I told her.

'Daddy,' she said again and this time something wavered in
her voice. Something he recognized.

'Where are you?' he said.

There was sniffing. A choking back.

'Where are you?'

'I need to come home,' she said.

He wanted to say it. I told you so. Say it and feel better, he
thought. Say it and show her you won. But she was not there
to fight. He could hear something else. So he let it fall though
he had it all right there loaded and ready to fire since he didn't
know how many years. Two or three or maybe four. She said
it again. I need to come home and I'm coming right now. A
click and then nothing.

As soon as he set down the phone he had the memory of his daughter getting into a fender bender just after receiving her license. She hadn't been wearing her seatbelt and she had smacked her head hard against the windshield, bringing blood that was matted in her hair when he picked her up at the emergency room. The wreck had been her fault and as they drove toward home he kept asking her what happened but she didn't want to talk about it. And when they got home both knelt over the side of the bathtub and he helped her wash the blood out of her hair and then after she had wrapped her hair in a towel and sat on the edge of the tub, as he was walking out of the bathroom she said I wish mama was here. It was the first time in her life she had said it to him.

I wish mama was here.

So do I.

That's all it would have taken, he thought. Three words. Not even those three. Any three would have answered her and closed the evergrowing gap between father and daughter and she had been reaching for him in that moment. He knew it then and he knew it now and he had only slipped into the kitchen and poured from the bottle.

He crossed the kitchen and did the same thing as he had done the day he left her alone in the bathroom. He opened the cabinet and took out the bourbon but he only set it on the counter. Did not open it. He stared at the bottle and touched his fingertip to the curve in the neck. Squeezed his eyes shut. Then he opened his eyes and returned the bottle to the shelf and slammed the cabinet door.

He walked outside. In all directions the yellowbrown cornstalks swayed in the wind, their leaves a rustling chorus of thousands. No harvest in the last three years as the storms brought the rainfall and the rainfall drenched the fields and the fields never had time to dry out and the stalks had quit giving. The acres surrounding the house stood as swaying and mocking reminders and he would have long since cut them to nubs if the combine could navigate the soggy earth but it couldn't. All he could do was look at it. And wait for her.

7

It took two hours to drive to her father's house. Moving along two-lane roads that passed through small towns decorated with signs that read for sale or going out of business or no trespassing. Lumberyards and grain mills sat silent and rusting as industrial relics of sundrenched times and rows of FEMA trailers lined the parking lots of empty strip malls where children stood with backpacks and lunchboxes waiting on the school bus.

A soggy landscape below. Clouds pushing across the sky above. The hatchback crossed from Louisiana into Mississippi and she felt something turn inside her as she passed the windbent WELCOME TO MISSISSIPPI sign on Highway 61. Jace slept on the passenger seat, curled into a ball and covered with her jacket. She had found two cigarettes in a pack on the floorboard and she was finishing the second one as she turned east on Highway 24 and began to recognize the names of towns. Woodville, then Centreville, then Liberty. Hitting the backroads in Liberty and snaking through the hills and valleys. Passing no one and seeing no one and she imagined the rough strip of asphalt going on and on and on until the car would simply run out of gas and that was just it. No world left to engage, only the end of the road. Jace coughed and sat up. Once more stared at her with wonder. She stroked the fine hair of the back of his head and then he lay back down and he was asleep again as she made the final turn toward home.

8

WADE WAS SITTING ON THE steps of the front porch wearing a thick flannel coat when the hatchback turned onto the dirt road, moving slowly between the crops and then rolling to a stop in the yard. He stood and stepped down and walked toward the car. She shifted into park and killed the ignition and she sat there behind the wheel. They studied one another.

Then Jace sat up in the passenger seat. The top of his head catching Wade's attention. Jessie looked over to the boy and he crawled over the seat and into her lap. She wrapped her arms around him. Held him. Stared back at Wade.

Wade moved around the side of the car and opened the door. She got out holding the boy, who raised his sleepy eyes to Wade and then dropped his head against his mother's chest.

'Who is that?' Wade asked.

'It's Jace.'

'Where'd he come from?'

'The same place every baby comes from.'

'You know what I mean.'

'And you already know the answer.'

She walked past him and up the steps and into the house. Wade looked around as if someone else may get out of the car and explain things to him. He shut the car door and he climbed the steps and sat down again. Lighting a cigarette and watching the cornstalks move in the wind and then the understanding that his daughter had a baby moving over him in the same manner. She didn't even tell you. And he ain't even a baby anymore. She had a baby and didn't tell you and now the baby is a boy and she didn't even tell you.

He heard the toilet flush inside the house. Footsteps back across the floor. A small cry. The words of a mother consoling a child. The cry diminishing. The door opening. He smoked and grew nervous as if whatever she was about to come out of the house and tell him was his fault.

She sat down next to him on the steps and Jace sat between them. Wade looked down at the small boy and the boy raised his finger and pointed at him.

'That's Wade,' Jessie told him.

Wade took the end of his little finger and shook it.

'And that's Jace,' she said to her father.

'Jace,' he said. 'That's a good name.'

'You got another cigarette?'

He reached into his shirt pocket and handed her his pack and a lighter.

'You're too young to be smoking,' he said.

She laughed a little. Cupped her hands and blocked the wind and got it lit and then she took a long drag.

'I wish there was some way to make you realize just how old I am. If anybody should know that then you should know it. Maybe one day my age and your age will settle where you think they're supposed to be but this ain't the day.'

Jace babbled. They smoked and watched the wind.

'Where is Holt?' Wade said.

'I can't believe you said his name.'

'Where is he?'

'I don't know.'

'You don't know.'

'That's what I said.'

'It must be bad.'

'What must be bad?'

'Everything.'

'Gee, Dad. You think?'

'I can't figure why else you'd be here.'

'Well. There you go.'

Wade sucked his cigarette down to the butt and he flicked it into the yard and then when he started to talk again she stopped him.

'I don't have it in me right now,' she said. 'I'm hungry. He's hungry. I'm tired. He's tired. We're here. That's all that matters. I swear to God all I want to do is eat and get clean and go lay down. Can we just do that?'

Wade nodded. Stood from the steps. He held out his hand and she took it and he helped her up. Jace got to his feet and she told him to come on. Let's go find something to eat. And he let out a quick and happy cry and then hustled between Jessie and Wade as they went inside and closed the door against the biting wind.

9

THREE YEARS BEFORE HOLT HAD awakened with his face in the dirt, out behind a cinderblock bar on the outskirts of St. Francisville. A deepdrunk night that held no details and his mouth dry and chalky and he raised his ringing head, gravel stuck to the side of his face and his head damp with drunksweat. Across the empty field that reached from the parking lot, a great white tent was being erected. He got to his feet. Wiped the gravel from his face and meandered across the field toward the gathering of men and women working to raise the tent, drifting in some mindless and staggered gait as if he were not only still drunk but also trapped in a lucid dream of beckoning.

A sloppy circle of vehicles surrounded the work. A couple of RVs and a station wagon and a handful of pickup trucks towing trailers. Parked out to the side of them all was a black hearse with a foothigh cross erected on the hood and as Holt staggered across the uneven field, tripping once and going down and then rising from the high grass and moving again, the sun split the clouds and shined down onto the hearse and it seemed to him in his hurting and bloated head that there was some kind of miracle occurring in this moment and if he could only make it across the field and to the gathering of people who were working in a quiet cooperation of raising the tent of praise then his life may somehow finally be worth a shit.

He made it there. They worked on the tent and moved in and out of vehicles and nobody said a word to him. He stood there, wiping dirt from the side of his face and neck. Hurting and alone. The side of his pants and shirt where he passed out in the parking lot lathered in red dirt. A little blood on the sleeve of his shirt from he didn't know what. A man in a cowboy hat was driving thick spikes into the ground around the edges of the tent. The bang bang bang of steel against steel, each strike like a hard jab into the throbbing of his hangover. The man rose and saw him and Holt halfwaved and the man stared at him. Shook his head. Moved on to the next spike and banged again.

And then he saw the driver's side door of the hearse open and she stepped out into the sunshine and his faith in a miracle was restored as she walked right under the tent as three men pushed against a center pole and the top rose toward the sky, as if she had been waiting for the very moment of ascension before making her appearance. She then walked right past the man with the cowboy hat who said something to her and right past a woman with a bad limp who bowed her head in reverence as the hardlooking woman moved beyond her and toward Holt who watched her with bloodshot eyes as she crossed the field and came right up to him and before he could utter a word or even a sound, she reached up and touched the scars on the back of his neck as if she had always known him and always known his scars and she said I have been waiting for you to find your way home.

She was a small and wiry woman with smokestained teeth and roadmap skin but she carried the weight of a much larger presence. She stared up at Holt as she ran her bony fingers across the scars of his neck and when she asked if he wanted to join the flock, he nodded and followed her back across the field and to the tent which now stood taut. Men erected a makeshift pulpit and women set out folding chairs and she walked him from one worker to the next and introduced him not by name but as the new lamb and they nodded to him and shook his hand and by the time the curious souls of the sparse community began to wander toward the tent as the organ music echoed through the hard wind of an approaching storm, he had put on a clean shirt and wiped the gravel from his hair and ear and he was standing with the wicker basket in front of the pulpit where Elser pumped and praised. When she gave the spiritual last call the congregation stood and began to form a line and reach into their pockets as they one by one stopped in front of Holt and dropped whatever money they had into the wicker basket.

The sermons that Elser delivered under the tent of the Temple of Pain and Glory were filled with hellfire and damnation. A doctrine that camouflaged a more pure theology of greed and dread and lust. A mindfuck of religion. The tent revival and its aggressive and chainsmoking leader doled out salvation to dilapidated, barely governed communities across Louisiana and Mississippi, places where the population seemed to dwindle each day, but the revival arrived anyway and offered up sizzling hallelujahs and praise-the-lords from a castiron skillet of fear and loathing.

Holt didn't believe a word of it. He did what he was supposed to do in the setup and breakdown and when it was his turn to take the offering he took the offering. When the out-of-tune organ began to play he would sit down in a chair in the back of the congregation, the chair legs sucked into the soggy earth. Sometimes the rain tapped against the tent and Elser cranked up the microphone to its highest level and her voice seemed to arise from some great hole of desperation and other times the sky was clear and the dusk came with the song of the cicadas and Elser knew she had the clarity of sound that she needed and her voice came hard and sharp and fast as if she may spring from the pulpit at any second and pour the blood of Christ right down your throat.

The Gulf Coast region had begun to take on a hurricane every few months. There was no longer an off season. And each time a storm pushed through and flooded the areas that had barely dried out from the last flooding, Holt believed that would be the end of the revival. More people evacuated and fewer returned. The big grocery stores closed. The car dealerships left vacant lots. There were long lines at whatever bank branch remained open. Longer lines at the liquor stores. Schools functioned with makeshift faculty, sometimes patching grades together. Baton Rouge and New Orleans took on the people who believed that a bigger place was somehow safe from the storms but the bigger places turned into infestations of crime and poverty while the smaller towns trudged along in a stitchwork of government and services.

No storm could deter the Temple. Elser and her crew would ride out the hurricane in some strip of motel rooms outside of Ferriday or Tylertown, playing cards and smoking anything they could find to smoke and drinking and sleeping and joining hands in hungover prayer when it felt like the motel might get clobbered.

On the back end of the storms, the sun always shined. Sometimes for weeks. Bright blue days with a high sun and high temps and Elser would get them all back into the vehicles and they would hit the road. She never told them where they were going. Only to follow. Once Holt asked Elser as she was getting in the hearse what direction they were headed and before Elser could answer the organist yelled from across the parking don't worry about it.

He didn't worry about it. But Holt began to watch the congregation more closely. The dwindling numbers. People who had lost their livelihoods and could lose their lives by remaining in the region but here they were anyway. No matter the field or parking lot or beatup town the Temple of Pain and Glory raised its banner. The people appeared and they listened to Elser rant and rave and they clapped as they sang and she promised each and every lost soul that their body and spirit were in the right place. There was no weather report or news story that could have driven these people from the dangers of the stormravaged land and Elser knew it. She berated them for even thinking of leaving. You can't trust *Them*. You can't listen to *Them*. *They* don't know what the weather is going to do, only God above knows what the weather is going to do and do you think your God would forsake you? Would drown you? Would wash you down the river and straight to hell? Even though you deserve it as the sinners you are. Even though you have doubt and even though you want to believe *Them* and you want to listen to the people with the radars and technology, only God knows. Holt watched as they clapped at such proclamations, Elser's message not so difficult to deliver as their minds about who they were and what they were and what they deserved had been made up generations ago. She beat them with the stick of distrust and they cheered their own suffering.

Holt could no longer look at their eyes when he was holding the wicker basket. The weather getting worse and he saw people with almost nothing giving everything they had to a cause that had no definition. He kept his head down as they pulled wet and crumpled dollar bills from shirt pockets and coin purses. And Elser rode it harder each revival. *Them,* she alluded to more often. The storms are a product not of God, but of *Them,* because *They* want the storms and the devastation, *They* want the dilapidation, *They* want the suffering. *They* don't want your precious white blood to prosper, *They* want you to join the herd and rise up out of the torrents not by spiritual revival but by upheaval, by taking your family and leaving your home and your possessions and running into the firepit of sin that burns inside the herd. *They* are full of untruth and *They* want you to forsake who you are and what you are for higher ground but how can *They* speak to you of higher ground when the spiritual life of the herd is milling about on the bottom of a soulless ocean.

She began to transform into something more dynamic. Sharper. More combative. Her sermons began with notions of sacrifice and sharing. Jesus healing the lepers. The feeding of the thousands with the fishes and the loaves. Moses leading his people through the parting of the Red Sea. But in the course of gaining the attention of the congregation, the sermons morphed into savage interrogations. She would take the microphone from the pulpit and walk down into the crowd, something she had never done in the first months that Holt was with the revival. She would clutch the microphone with both hands, her small knuckles turning white as she squeezed and her face turning red as her eyes bulged and she moved down the aisle and through the rows and she leaned close to them and screamed out her questions. Do you want to be swallowed in the Red Sea and drowned with the saltwater of sin? Is that what you want? Do you want to taste the miracle of Jesus? Do you think you deserve it? Do you think any of those people on the hillside deserved to eat one bite of the holy fish and bread? Do you think they earned it? Do you? The parishioners would rock back in their chairs at her first attack. Surprised. Big eyes. Scared. But it never failed, no matter the shock of Elser's delivery, no matter how close her finger came to poking someone in the face, no matter how hard she ridiculed their pathetic and sinlaced lives, eventually the shouts came in support of the righteous condemnations as she heaved threats right into the tired eyes of the locals who had suffered so much already.

Do you want to die where *They* tell you to die or do you want to live where the rain can wash away your sin? Do you believe that any of *Them* love you and love the Lord like I love the Lord? Do you believe that your soul is covered in leprosy? Do you know why it has not healed of the sores and the pus? Did you know it's your fault because of your wanting to accept what *They* tell you about this place only you can know as home? Do you believe that where the sun shines *They* are getting what *They* don't deserve? *They* are getting what belongs to you? Do you believe me or do you believe *Them*?

All the questions and all the pressure and all the screaming doubled the offering. Holt marveled at the congregation and its appetite for severity. It didn't matter if it was two hundred people in Clinton, Louisiana, or twenty people in Gloster, Mississippi, or anything in between. The Temple of Pain and Glory kept weathering the storm and kept trolling back and forth across the state lines and kept raising the tent and kept hurling the rocks of judgment and kept filling the wicker basket.

But then Elser surprised them all again.

A starstruck night in Bogalusa. A great humidity. Underneath the tent the tinywinged insects swarmed in the lights of revival and Elser dripped with sweat and the congregation dripped with sweat as she had whipped the service into a righteous frenzy. She howled in the aisles and they howled back and then she did like she always did after bombarding the congregation, returning to the pulpit while the adrenaline was flowing and calling for the wicker basket to make its way to its customary spot in front. It was Holt's turn and he walked over and stopped below the podium. Stood politely. He looked out at the men and women and children who believed they had been treated special. And then he waited for her to begin her call for the offering.

She didn't. Instead she began to speak of a tall tale about this little girl who controlled the weather. This *child,* she said. A murmur went through the crowd. This promised child, she said. The congregation crooned. Heads turned. Eyes catching. Did we hear that right?

Elser continued. She asked them if anyone was aware of the promise of this child or if perhaps God had spoken to her alone. Can anyone testify? Has anyone seen the vision or felt the call of the voice of the Lord while you were hunkered down listening to the wind whip and the thunder bellow?

A hesitant hand went up in the back. Then another. A dozen hands rose.

Hallelujah, Elser said. Hallelujah. I dreamed of this child. This promise. This little girl who can deliver us from the rumble of the almighty storms. It was a dream of the world come back around, needing another child, this child that is out there somewhere. In my dream the voice of God spoke to me and told me of her ability to command the skies, the ability to communicate with Mother Nature, the ability to return our region to prosperity and to the glory of early days. But our God above said to me that this holy child, being pure and clean and full of the testament of God and His might, has been stolen and hidden away because *They* want to keep us on our knees. And we must believe and pray and give and give and give until this child, the beautiful little girl, appears to us and raises her gentle hands that carry the power of miracles and calm these skies and these seas and make us whole again.

Holt had turned around and was facing Elser. Astonished by the ambition of this prophecy. And the congregation had gone silent and still. Their mouths agape and the idea and the hope of a second coming funneling down their throats.

Elser looked down at Holt and spoke right to him. This child will save us and we will find her. But only if we have every resource available to us. I plead for every single one of your prayers and for your contribution made in faith, no matter how great or small. Now come forward and fill the basket with the blessings our God has given unto you, every dollar is a blessing and it will take the culmination of all of our blessings to rescue the child from *Them* and allow God to speak through her abilities to return us to the light and send the black clouds back into the recesses of the skies where they belong.

She raised her eyes from Holt and looked across the congregation. The believers were already merging toward the aisle. They came and they gave. They gave so much another revival worker had to join Holt with another basket. The organ played and the insects swarmed in the yellow light and the parishioners circled back around to their seats after giving it all and Holt had to press the mob of cash down when it overflowed and as the organ played a closing hymn and as the voices joined together to sing of cloudless days and streets of gold, Holt turned around to the pulpit to look at Elser, wanting to see the smear of satisfaction across her face. But she was not there. She had stepped down from the pulpit and walked out of the tent and into the darkness, leaving them singing and crying out for the child who would give them back their world.

10

WADE MADE THEM SCRAMBLED EGGS and it was gone in an instant and then he made them some more. As they ate the second round he built a fire in the fireplace and outside the light sunk away into the damp earth. When Jessie was done eating she slumped in the kitchen chair with a full belly and her head began to nod in exhaustion. He told her to get up and go on to bed but she said I have to get clean. I'll sleep so much better. She took Jace with her into the bathroom and washed him first in the tub and he became a clean little man with toweldried hair. She strapped a diaper on him and nudged him out of the bathroom and she turned on the shower and closed the door.

Jace came over to Wade who was sitting on the hearth. The fire popping and beginning to warm the room. Jace leaned against Wade's knee and Wade looked at him curiously. He saw the resemblance to Jessie across the boy's eyes and nose and when Jace kept mumbling and pointing at the flames, Wade picked him up.

'Fire,' Wade said.

'Fi,' Jace repeated.

The boy smelled like soap and youth. The aroma of a life yet to be lived. Wade breathed it in as if it had some restorative power, closing his eyes and closing his mouth and sucking in through his nostrils.

'Fi,' Jace said again.

Wade carried him into the bedroom and found a clean t-shirt and he put it on the boy. It gathered on the floor around Jace's feet and Wade bunched it together and made a knot in the back. Photographs hung on the woodpanel wall in a sporadic pattern as if hung blindly and Jace pointed at the frames. Rebecca and Wade sitting on a tailgate in the year before they married, beers in hand. Rebecca in a cowboy hat standing next to a horse. An infant Jessie sleeping with her thumb in her mouth. Six-year-old Jessie riding piggyback on her father. A series of school photographs spanning Jessie's childhood and into her teen years, placid posturing against various shaded and generic backdrops. In some photographs she smiled and in others her mouth bent in a forced grin as if trying to conceal some possible eruption. The only photograph that was without a frame was that of a setting sun across a wave of hillside that cut through the trees and splintered orange across the land and it was held to the wall with a thumbtack.

Wade set the boy down and picked up the room, shoving clothes from the bed and floor into the closet. He bent over and smelled the sheets and then stripped off the sheets and pillowcases and found blankets in the hall closet and spread them across the mattress. Jace milled about the room, picking shotgun shells out of an open box in the corner and then reaching for the shotgun leaning in the corner. Wade snatched the weapon and stuck it in the closet behind the hanging clothes and jackets and shut the closet door. He then scooped up the boy and as they passed the bathroom, Jessie was singing over the drone of the shower.

Jessie and Jace slept in Wade's room on the full bed and he lay in what had been her room on the old twin mattress under the window. Wide awake. The window without a curtain, ripped down by Jessie long ago in some fit of youthful rage. The closet door open and a scattering of clothes on hangers and on the floor. The way she had left it years ago as she snatched shirts and shoes and whatever else she could cram into a bag before she stormed out of the house and across the yard and climbed into the car with the man Wade hated. The man with the scars on his neck. The man too old for her who didn't talk and didn't listen when Wade told him to stop coming around and didn't do anything but stare back at Wade from behind the steering wheel before driving away with his daughter. Posters still hung on the wall of beautiful teenagers striking beautiful poses and strands of Mardi Gras beads hung on a nail. In the top drawer of her small dresser there was a drawing of a mother and daughter that Jessie had created in art class in third grade.

He hadn't even known that dying in childbirth happened anymore, believing it was for more primitive times. Something for old weathered mothers with old weathered headstones. But it happened in a room in a hospital with electric lights and linoleum floors and beeping machines and doctors and nurses and dozens of years of medical schooling and experience. She's lost a lot of blood the doctor had said and then he said a lot of other things that Wade didn't listen to. All he could hear was she has lost a lot of blood. When the doctor finally paused Wade said if she's lost a lot of blood then stop it. Don't let her lose any more. We're trying, the doctor said. Then stop trying and goddamn do it. Get in there and do it and quit coming out here and telling me all this bullshit while she's in there losing blood. Get the hell in there and stop it. Goddamn do it. The doctor had gone back in and Wade paced up and down the hallway and then it happened to Rebecca with him right outside the room, listening to the screaming and the hustle of nurses in and out and then no more screaming. The long stretch of a deep and hurtful silence was finally interrupted with a slap and then another slap and then a tiny wail. Life and death passing one another like strangers. And then the child was placed in his arms and he held her and looked into the eyes that were awaking to the world and he knew right then that it was going to be hard and that he wasn't ready for it and that he would fail her.

And now here she was again. Barely eighteen the day she left but so different from that now. Asleep in the other room with her own child. She was thinner than she should have been. Experience in her eyes. She was different but she was here. He tried to figure out how long it had been and he was ashamed that he didn't know. That he wasn't even certain how old she was. Was it twentyone or twentytwo?

He listened to the wind. He closed his eyes. He tried to sleep. But each time he reached the edge of slumber he was roused by the image of redeyed wolves stalking through the dark. Creeping toward the door.

11

IT WENT FROM BAD TO worse for Wade after Jessie ran off. All of it. The drinking and the loneliness and the self-imposed isolation. And then the work began to fall away as hurricanes became more frequent, brutal storms driving into the Gulf again and again. In between the hurricanes came long bouts of drought or endless rains. Seldom an in-between. None of it helpful to the crops that either starved or drowned and he wasn't needed to work the big machinery except in random jobs on random farms where in fleeting moments there was work to be done. The harvests fell away and then the offshore oil rigs began to shut down. No way to withstand the more frequent stream of storms. He got a small severance check from the offshore company which he thought would be fine to hold him over until he found another job but there never came another job. Corporations shut down businesses across Mississippi and Louisiana. The population shrank. Local stores closed. No one was hiring and no one with any money to sink into the region was willing to pretend the shift in weather was a hoax.

But the liquor stores stayed open and he drank and drove around and drank some more and smoked cigarettes and built fires in the fireplace and drank some more and watched his severance pay dwindle and he drove around and drank some more and slept whenever he wanted and woke up and did it all again. Living in a steady stupor. Running out of money and no longer trying and wondering where his daughter was and on the bad nights holding a blade to his own throat as he stood outside with the wind howling and the clouds rushing across the sky. Rising with his head pounding and eyes puffed and bloodshot and standing in the shower and watching the water swirl down the drain and promising himself that's it. Enough of this shit. And then by the afternoon finding any combination of nickels and quarters and dollars and driving back to the liquor store.

It was down to Night Train or Mad Dog by then. The bottles on the bottom shelf. And when he couldn't come up with two or three dollars he went in with whatever pocket change he could muster and begged Billy to let him have a bottle and let him owe the difference because if he didn't get the bottle he knew the next step was to end up on the highway that carried him to the rolling hills in the wide open country where he would find the trailer sitting back off the road and follow the gravel that wound between trees and into the open field where the trailer sat like some bitter island and then he would turn to meth because the trailer would take a trade. The trade of anything. Flesh. Blood. Whatever. Because once the trailer had you there was no going back and he did not want to go to the trailer and he did not want the rotting teeth and sunk jaw and skintface look of the walking dead and so he would beg Billy to let him have a bottle of anything. Goddamn anything. Anything to keep him from the road out of town that led to the gravel road that led to the trailer and he knew he would end up there.

The day that Billy wouldn't front him another bottle and his wheels turned onto the gravel and the trees bent in the hard wind, he rolled on toward the trailer as if he was rolling on toward his own grave. When he saw the trailer and he saw the shirtless man standing outside and wearing rubber gloves that reached to the elbows, all the goddamn hell that was left to suffer rose up and squeezed his cheeks and said of all the things you do not want I can promise you this is at the top of the list. The wind blew and he stopped the truck and stared at the trailer and then he shifted into park. Then shifted into reverse. And he turned around in the grass and drove away from the trailer and drove back toward home along the highway.

He shook and shivered and puked for days upon days but he never drank another drop and never once drove on the highway toward the trailer and he sometimes thought he would give his soul for one last pint of bourbon or vodka or tequila or anything that would let him fly away into the swirling and lifting worlds of inebriation but he only closed his eyes and made hard fists and batted at his own forehead in the fierce action of combat of one man against himself.

But was still alone. And he had to eat.

He had spied an abandoned cattle trailer in a field a couple of miles down the road. He kept his eyes on it for weeks and then he finally decided to take it. He hitched it to his truck and brought it home. Fortified the rusted bottom with plywood. Rewired it so the taillights worked. And then he began to drive down across the state line and into Louisiana, into the dilapidated communities where houses and apartments sat silently. Some with roofs covered in blue tarps. Some with no roofs. Some with no damage at all, only left behind before the damage came. He took the heating and cooling units from the houses and apartments and loaded them into the cattle trailer and then he drove a couple of hours north to salvage yards in Byram and Brandon and wherever else he could find a salvage yard that paid cash for scrap. He never ran out. So many gone across the Mississippi and Louisiana border. So much left behind. Sometimes he thought of it as stealing. Sometimes he thought of it as recycling. All the time he thought of it as survival.

12

WHEN ELSER WAS A CHILD she had been prone to episodes of detachment. Instances where her eyes would lose their attention on whatever was at hand and rise and look out before her into some dim and private realm that only she could see. Her body still. Her expression tranquil. An escape from the physical world. During these episodes she would not respond to anyone or anything as she remained in this hypnotic state until she was ready to come out of it and once her eyes livened and reengaged she could not remember having been under such a spell.

Her mother believed that in these moments her daughter was experiencing holy visions. That she was a child with special gifts. That she was a child in dialogue with God in the same way that God had spoken to other mortals through burning bushes or raging seas or dreams of feast or famine. Her mother ignored what the school nurses suggested about Elser's episodes. She ignored what the doctors suggested when Elser's eyes rolled back in her head when God could have only been delivering a most potent message and there was no choice but to lift the girl and throw her in the backseat and drive like hell to the emergency room. She ignored what people she knew said to her about it at the laundromat or at the bar because she was convinced she had a daughter with special gifts and those with special gifts can neither be understood nor diagnosed.

Elser's mother wore her hair long, reaching to the small of her back. It was thin and stayed tangled as if she was caught in a perpetual whirlwind and her eyes were green and bold like bursts of spring. A crazed and disheveled look that caused heads to turn away in grocery aisles and bank lines and anywhere else the good people moved about. She was a woman with her own demons, in a steady conversation with herself where voices came out of her in multiple tones and with multiple accents and the steady babble created a selective hearing in young Elser as she learned to tune out her mother and her chatter. They moved in and out of apartments and in and out of towns with their lives fitting into a handful of boxes that could be packed and loaded in less than an hour if that was the necessity.

Her mother shifted through stages. There was great indulgence of food and drink when piles of junk food in cellophane wrappers lay scattered across the kitchen counter and the refrigerator was filled with quarts of beer and two-liters of Coke. During the indulgence there were men and more men and chainsmoking and nights when the television never turned off and her mother's eyes never closed and the voices that leapt from her were more combative and threatening. During these stretches Elser stayed in her room if she had her own and if she didn't have her own she would stay outside until dark and then find the most quiet corner of the apartment where she would sit with the Bible open across her lap and she would read the Old Testament. Nightly homework from her mother. She was to look for clues into the conversations between man and God, the same kind of conversations her mother was certain she was having. Elser read the ancient tales and tried to understand how to look for the signs of impending doom and promises of wrath and she tried to figure how to relay the messages she had received during her visionary episodes. Messages she could not remember but messages that her mother explained were important to the fate of mankind.

Her mother's stretches of indulgence were always followed by long reaches of cleansing where there was little food and no sugar and no caffeine and no explanation and her mother and her voices were not happy until her mother had shriveled to skin and bone. So Elser shriveled to skin and bone. She would sneak food from the cafeteria trays of classmates and shove halfeaten rolls and chicken strips into her pockets to take home so she could eat again before it was time to return to the cafeteria the next day. She hid scraps of food in her pillowcase on Fridays so she could eat over the weekend. With her mother's wild swings the child learned extremes and the depths of emotions that come with them and at an early age the idea was manifested in her that extremity was normal. Nothing that came without risk or sacrifice was worth the time of day.

She also learned to lie. When Elser would come out of one of her episodes or a teacher told her mother that she had one at school, the interrogation began. Her mother would sit with her on the floor and lean close to her face and lather her with questions. What did you see? Was it the future? Was it the past? Was there fire and wind and rain? Did you walk through heaven? Was God speaking to you like you were a child or like you were one of his prophets? Have you seen the devil? What did he look like? Did he touch you? Was Jesus there? What did he tell you? Answer me. You can't keep all this shit to yourself. You have to answer me.

In the beginning Elser was frightened by her mother's inquisition. She cried. She pulled away. She was confused and frightened. But then she learned how to make the questions go away. By answering them. She started by nodding or shaking her head when she could. If that wouldn't do she would keep her answer to one or two words. This pacified her mother and her mother answered many of the questions herself by taking whatever suggestion Elser had given her and creating her own interpretation.

But then as time wore on, Elser had grown to become amused by the exchange. Her answers began to take the form of sentences and sometimes stories. Recollections of the dialogue between her and God. She told her mother of the heavens. She told her mother of the darkness in the eyes of Jesus when he mentioned Satan and his angels. And then she began to settle her messages into the everyday. We will see a stray dog and we are to go in the opposite direction to avoid harm. It will rain soon and this is a sign for us to remain in this apartment and not move again until I am given more instruction. There is a chosen child that is yet to be found that will do great things and I am to read the New Testament now to try and understand.

Is it you? her mother wanted to know. She would take her daughter by the shoulders and shake her. It has to be you. It has to I know it. It has to be.

When Elser was challenged to give her mother more specific answers to what she had learned from her vision, sometimes the spiritual adrenaline reached such a peak that she did feel as if she held some special knowledge of the unanswerable. At other times when she was less spirited she delivered exactly what her mother wanted to hear in a less dramatic but matter-of-fact precision and she learned to navigate between the two deliveries like a seasoned orator of oldtime religion.

And though she had found comfort in her ability to manipulate her mother and the choices she made, what remained of her childhood innocence was worn with the guilt that came from trying to decide if her prophetic personality was a sin or if it was simply a path into a manageable existence. In time the guilt manifested itself into conviction. I do see, she came to believe. And I do know things that no one else can know. And I can do whatever I want to do with this ability.

It's mine.

It was with that conviction that at the age of fifteen she stuffed her meager belongings into a grocery bag. She grabbed her Bible and what was left of a pack of cigarettes. Her mother lay passed out in the bed. Two men lay passed out beside her. The season of indulgence was upon them. Her mother was no longer her mother to her, only some irritation to work around to get what you want. She slung the bag over her shoulder and leaned in the bedroom doorway and she stared at the sleeping and snoring flops of flesh. The last thing she said to her mother before she turned and left and walked out the door was I have seen the fires of hell. And you dance among the flames.

13

From the moment Elser introduced the child into the end of the sermon, Holt began to pay attention to the service. No more wandering away from the tent, smoking cigarettes and sipping from a halfpint. No more wandering into whatever wornout town in hopes of finding a neon light and a willing woman. Now he sat in a chair at the back of the tent with his eyes glued to Elser. The anticipation filling him, waiting to see if she would tell the story of the little girl. The flesh and blood of God himself.

She did not disappoint. After making her rounds through the audience lambasting the sinners, she would return to the podium. Catch her breath. Take a handkerchief from her pocket and wipe the sweat from her face. Sometimes now she even lit a cigarette. She would wait until the temper of the congregation calmed from her previous ferocity. And then she would lower her eyes and deepen her tone and begin with the same four words each time, spoken just above a whisper, her lips touching the microphone.

There is a child.

A long pause followed. Holt would sit up in his chair, though he had heard it the night before and the night before that. A little girl, Elser would continue. A little girl who has the ability to control the weather. God's long-awaited return to earth. And this child, she is out there. Somewhere. If only we can find this heavenly gift, then your life will be restored.

She had them. The small, wrinkled, lightweight monster of a woman had them. Whether any of the throng actually believed her proclamation, Holt couldn't tell. But he could see that they wanted to. They gawked and nodded and raised their hands and whispered prayers and called out to God for the discovery of His child and some cried and some collapsed to their knees and some did all of it. Elser continued the practice of ducking out of the back of the tent while the offering was being gathered and the last hymn played. Before the story of the child, she had always stayed and spoken with members of the congregation after the service. They wanted to talk to her. They wanted to introduce her to a family member stricken by a humped back or riddled with the sunkjaw and rotting teeth of bad habits, believing Elser's blotchy hands could heal or that her words may be like some restorative scripture forever engraved upon their souls. They wanted more. They always wanted more.

Her disappearance from the pulpit set the parishioners to talking the moment the last note of the final hymn was struck and their talk continued when they got home and when they spoke to someone on the telephone or saw them at the gas station and it wasn't long before the crowds began to grow again, people driving from one or two towns over to sit beneath the tent of the Temple of Pain and Glory and hear firsthand the divination of the chosen child. Holt heard them questioning one another before the service. Have you heard? Do you know about the child? Yes, we heard. Do you believe it? I don't know, do you? I don't know.

The crowd grew so large at post-hurricane revivals that Elser had to buy the crew another truck to carry all the extra chairs. It now took two workers with wicker baskets to take the offering. If she could find them, Elser bought the crew steaks to grill on setup days instead of skinny pork chops. Holt had begun to wonder if joining Elser's flock, a flock that fed him and paid him and gave him a dry place to sleep on a bunk inside an RV, was the best thing that had happened to him. Or the worst.

Sometimes he believed the story of the little girl. Why not? Every other Bible story he had heard was the thing of fairy tales. Or nightmares. The innocent fed to lions. The innocent suffering plague and famine. The innocent nailed to a cross. A dead man rising from the grave. As he sat in his chair and listened to the tales he sensed that they were a blend of the movies and grandma stories and superstition and maybe religion. And if Elser could claim that such stories from the word of the living God were true and if the crowd could cheer and clap their hands and shout affirmation and if God could give commands through a burning bush or send a whale to swallow a man and spit him out at the beachfront of salvation then why the hell couldn't there be a miraculous little girl hidden in some house or cave or basement along the Mississippi-Louisiana line.

And then one day as they wrestled down the tent on the edge of a violent thunderstorm, as the wind whipped the ropes from the stakes and the tent flipped and flopped in the slanting rain while they tried to flatten it and wrangle it into some kind of makeshift ball the men could cram into the back of a truck, as Holt was whipped in the side of the head by one of the wayward ropes it turned his eyes toward the hearse where Elser sat behind the wheel. Smoking a cigarette. The world outside oblivious to her as the men fought the weather and the tent and the women gathered chairs and tables and rushed them to a trailer bed. Holt dropped what he was doing and walked toward the hearse as the men screamed at him to get back and grab the fucking rope and for Christ's sake don't run off. The rain and wind hard against him as he ignored their cries and leaned against the wind and moved closer to the hearse. The tip of her cigarette an orange spot in the gray storm and the cab filled with smoke as she stared at something she held on top of the steering wheel. Holt crept to the window and looked in and she never noticed him. Never took her eyes from the map she held and studied. The cigarette dangling from the corner of her mouth and a pen held between her fingers and little symbols dotting towns across the map of Louisiana and Mississippi. Stars and question marks and crosses and words he couldn't read through the smoke and rain.

He backed away from the hearse as the men struggled with the tent and he returned in no hurry as they barked at him to grab hold and help and as he snatched a rope and then grabbed the slick edge of the tent and worked with the others to harangue the tent into submission, the thought struck him like an electric shock. She's not moving the revival around to take their money.

She's looking for the child.

The door to the hearse opened and Elser stepped out the instant the realization crossed his mind, as if she had somehow been listening to the conversation in his head. She pushed the door closed and she began walking across the site as the workers fought against the storm but she kept her eyes on Holt. And he kept his eyes on her and the sound of the wind and rain and the shouts of working men and women all fell away as she walked in his direction.

He backed away from the wrestling with the tent. And he kept backing away as she came closer and then she held her hand up to signal him to stand still and he stood still. She stopped in front of him. He was a head taller than the woman but she carried a great certainty on her small frame.

'What?' she said.

Holt didn't answer. Shook his head in confusion.

'What do you want?' she said.

'I was just out here working.'

'I know that.'

'You came over here to me.'

'I also know that. But that's not what I asked you.'

'What did you ask me?'

'I asked you what you wanted.'

The rain slashed at their faces and hair and the wind pushed and the sky was growing darker and he had no idea.

'Why would you ask me that?' he said.

'Because.'

'Because why?'

'Because you seem to me to be different from the others.'

'What others?'

She reached and wiped the rain from his chin.

'You are heading for the dark,' she said.

He drew back his head.

'No,' he said. 'I can't be.'

'Why can't you?'

'Because I can't be headed for something I've already been standing in since before I started holding your money basket.'

'You shouldn't argue.'

'I ain't arguing.'

'Then if you know the dark then you should know what you want.'

'And what's that?'

'You should want out of it.'

Elser grinned. Lightning snapped and the wind gathered strength and trunk lids and trailer doors were starting to slam shut as the workers shoved the revival away and darted for cover inside their vehicles. She waved her hand toward the hostile sky and then she brushed her fingers across the scars on the side of his neck. She gazed at him and in the caverns of her eyes he felt some strange understanding and she said you don't yet know how deep the dark can be.

14

HOLT BEGAN TO NOTICE A stranger at the revival, from time to time and whenever they were setting up or breaking down. The man would appear on the site, seemingly out of nowhere as if he had formed from dust. And then he and Elser would talk a moment before going to the hearse and getting in and sitting together in conversation. Sometimes it was only a few minutes. Sometimes an hour. Every time the man got out and walked away without looking at or saying a word to any of the workers. Holt tried to follow him with his eyes as he departed, trying to see what vehicle he climbed into or if there were maybe others waiting on him but the man kept walking and walking until he either turned a corner or Holt put his attention to the work at hand and then looked up and he was simply gone.

The man was tall and wore a gray suit. The pants were too short and the coat was too baggy but he always wore the same thing. He carried a Bible and a notebook. He wore blackframe glasses and his face was lean and pale. Holt always watched him, waiting for the man to look in his direction. But Holt was always relieved when the man ignored him because behind the glasses were two deepset and grayrimmed eyes that scared him.

It was the tall man who gave the keys to Elser. Holt wasn't supposed to see it. He was taking a break from unloading tables and chairs, tucked behind a pickup and peeing in the grass when he heard the hearse doors open and Elser and the man climbed out. They walked a dozen steps away from the hearse and Holt zipped up and ducked down, spying on them with his eyes just above the truck bed. The man reached into his coat pocket and lifted out the keys. But they were not normal keys. The key ring was as round as a grapefruit and two hulking keys hung on the ring. They were big and black and looked like they opened the door to an ancient world. The man held them to Elser and spoke to her as if giving instructions. She smoked and listened and nodded. She didn't reach for them until he finished talking and then he held them to her. As she raised her hand to take them, he pulled them back. Said something else to her as if to reaffirm. She nodded again in understanding and then she took the ring from him and tucked it underneath her shirt.

That night Holt chased the tall and pale man all through his dreams. Sometimes the man would be walking along a sidewalk and Holt would be a block behind and he was running to try and catch up to the man but he could never gain any ground. Even when the man stopped to look into a storefront window and shift the knot of his tie or straighten his glasses, Holt could not catch him as if he were stuck on a treadmill. He woke in the middle of yelling at the man to stop right there and one of the others who shared the RV told him to shut the hell up. He tossed and turned but fell asleep again and this time the man walked through a marsh. Holt followed. The murky water kneehigh and the soggy bottom sucking at his feet as he struggled forward and after the man who seemed to be having no trouble at all navigating the mud and fallen limbs and crazed vines that turned and twisted through the dark trees. The marsh smelled rotten and was snakefilled and Holt slapped away the serpents that moved in silent curves across the blackwater and in his sleep he slapped at the mattress and again he was told to shut the hell up but he was chasing the man in his dreamworld. The man climbed out of the water and stood on a stump and this time Holt was able to close in on him, splashing and surging through the muck and as Holt reached the stump the man removed his glasses and stared down at Holt with those grayrimmed eyes and was just about to speak when Holt was smacked with a pillow and he was brought back into the darkness of the RV where a silhouette stood over him wielding the pillow and telling him to get still or get out.

He did not go back to sleep.

The next day Elser told them we're not going anywhere right now and she put the workers up in motel rooms and said she would be back in a few days. A few days turned into eight. In those nights in the motel room, Holt could not rest. When short bouts of sleep arrived he dreamed again of the tall man. He dreamed of the keys. He dreamed of streaks of lightning coming from Elser's fingertips as she zapped the Holy Spirit into any nonbeliever within range. And he dreamed of a little girl with dark eyes sitting alone in an empty room.

During the day he smoked and drank coffee and only nibbled at whatever sandwich and fries he ordered in whatever derelict town they were stuck in. By twilight he was drinking from a bottle of cheap bourbon and pacing around the motel parking lot and staring up at the dustblue sky, setting his eyes on the shifting clouds and concentrating all his energy into using his mind and spirit to move them this way or that way. But the clouds only went with the wind and he would mumble to himself. Bullshit. All of it. Bullshit. But in the middle of the night he would find himself in the parking lot again. Drunk now. Eyes on the moon. Concentrating again as he stared at the moonglow and tried to conjure a stormcloud to cover and dampen its light and when that didn't work he raised his arms and felt the nightbreeze and he closed his eyes and said a prayer to the god of the wind and begged for the breeze to rise but there was no answer. He said a prayer to the god of thunder but there was no rumble.

By the end of the eight days when Elser returned and walked the breezeway knocking on doors and telling them it was time to pack up and go, he had settled into a state of unravel. She saw him lumber from his motel room and toward his pickup, his bloodshot eyes and greasy hair and carrying his boots and walking barefoot across the rough parking lot. He looked as if he'd lost weight. As if he had been or still was sick. She met him at the truck and asked him what the hell was wrong.

He opened the door and tossed his boots and the clothes he carried inside the cab. He leaned over and spit. A milky drool ran down the side of his mouth and he wiped it on his shirtsleeve and he seemed as though he might be ready to fall over when he suddenly came to life. He looked at Elser and said you don't know anything. Do you?

The passenger door to the hearse opened. The tall man got out and crossed the parking lot. The man surprised Holt. He was not wearing his glasses and he stared at Holt with those deepset eyes. Holt swallowed hard and held straight and pursed his lips together as the man joined him and Elser at the truck door. The man looked at Elser and asked her if this was the one.

She took a step nearer to Holt. Put her face close to his and Holt leaned back a little. Then she turned to the tall man and nodded. Around them the other workers cranked engines and slammed doors and trunks and the revival vehicles hummed and revved in anticipation of the highway. Holt shifted his eyes between Elser and the tall man.

'Your soul is scarred,' she said. 'Like the scars you wear on your skin.'

The tension in Holt's expression fell away. He asked Elser to repeat what she had just said but Elser and the tall man only turned from Holt and walked back to the hearse. The hearse cranked and turned in the parking lot and moved out onto the highway and the revival caravan followed, vehicle after vehicle falling in line until Holt was left alone. He looked around the motel parking lot. Empty now but for one car. He climbed in the truck and slipped on his boots. He looked in the rearview mirror and then he ran his fingertips along the slick scars that stretched behind his neck. He lifted his shirt and felt their continuation across his back. He looked to the highway and the caravan had disappeared around a bend in the road.

15

A HEAVY NIGHT. THE AIR dripping with humidity and buzzing with mosquitoes and the wind came in gusts from all different directions. No pattern to its strength. The revival tent flapped and the ropes shook and in the near sky a lightning storm flashed from the depths of hulking clouds, the clouds in great gray silhouettes that shifted and shaped in the popping light like moving mountains. Beneath the tent there was sweat and singing and handclapping and proclamations, a hallelujah good time that was energized with each strike of whitehot light and boom of thunder. It was coming and they knew it and Elser berated them as a few members of the crowd slipped away, promising the flock that no storm was stronger than the power of the Holy Spirit and God will protect you from the wind and the water and they all raised their hands and said amen. A crash of thunder caused them all to turn their heads and look toward the stormfilled sky and then a strike of lightning split the clouds and splintered the dark and struck against the earth like the whip of God and they all let out a great gasp. Elser stopped. The organist stopped. Then from the back row a voice cried praise the Lord and the service cranked up again with such a fervor that a woman with a walker collapsed and two more grayhairs hit the ground before Elser could get done laying hands on the first one.

Away from the tent and out in the dark, Holt paced. He watched the lightning and smoked cigarettes and he held one of the steel spikes that was used to stake the tent. The grass was high and brushed against his boots as he shuffled back and forth. His forehead was damp with sweat and each time the sky lit up he paced a little quicker. He searched the grounds for the tall man but he had not appeared. The tent had been erected in a green space that stretched from a meager town hall to the railroad tracks, the rails rusted and weeds growing between the railroad ties and the revival vehicles and trailers and RVs sat gathered in the parking lot of what had once been the train station. All of the vehicles but Holt's truck, which sat parked three blocks away in an alleyway with the keys in the ignition. He didn't know the name of the town they were in but he knew this would be the last one he experienced with the Temple of Pain and Glory.

Your soul is scarred.

He paced and admired the fire in the sky and heard Elser's words repeating. Your soul is scarred. He heard the words and he felt the eyes of Elser and the tall man as they spoke to him so close, so quietly. So certainly. He wondered if she could truly see things that no one else could see. Another burst of lightning streaked from sky to earth and the wind howled and hats flew from heads and Holt tossed his cigarette and walked toward the vehicles.

Elser's small, boxlike RV was parked behind the hearse. One of the workers sat in a chair to guard the door, a development of recent weeks that spun Holt's curiosity. The man slouched and smoked and wore overalls with no shirt underneath and he stared slackjawed at the lightning storm. His slick hair unchanged in the wind. Holt stuck the spike into the back of his jeans as he approached him.

'What you think?' Holt said.

'About what?' he answered. His eyes remained on the carnival in the sky.

'About the storm. What else?'

'They ain't nothing new.'

'That lightning is new.'

'It's something indeed.'

The man then looked at Holt and Holt held his cigarette pack to him but the man shook him off. The music shifted into a more pulsing rhythm and the gospel clapping and singing echoed across the night.

'You need a break?' Holt asked.

'I ain't supposed to get up.'

'How come?'

'Cause Elser told me not to get up for nothing or nobody.'

'I ain't nobody. I work here.'

'She didn't say nothing about that.'

'I ain't worried what she said. I was just wondering if you needed a break.'

'I'm just sitting here. It ain't that hard.'

Holt sucked on his cigarette and then tossed it. Let out a great exhale and walked a little circle.

'I do have to piss,' the man said.

'All right. Go piss. I'll hold your seat.'

The man stood. Raised his arms and stretched. Scratched at his bare shoulder. Then he looked at Holt and turned serious.

'You listen to me,' he said. 'Not a soul goes in here. Not even the devil himself. That's exactly what Elser said.'

'There ain't even nobody out here.'

'You heard me. I'll be right back.'

The man slunk around the side of the RV. Holt watched him wander beyond the vehicles and into the dark. A big gust swept underneath the tent and a speaker and a stand crashed, the high pitch of feedback rang and people covered their ears and ducked their heads until one of the workers pulled the plug. Elser screamed into the microphone that no one could silence the word of God and the music kept on, amplified through the remaining windwobbling speakers.

Holt turned the handle on the RV but it was locked. He then pulled the spike from the back of his jeans. He listened to the music and got in rhythm and he struck down on the door handle on a high note. It didn't give. He tapped his foot and listened to the music and when the high note came again he struck the handle again and this time it busted. He pushed the door open and slipped inside and shut it behind him.

Dark and cramped. The dull light of the parking lot slipped between the blinds. He took out his lighter and flicked it and moved with the flame. A twin bed and shelves on one side. A table and kitchenette on the other. A closet dividing the space. Time was short and he was sloppy as he tore through the small camper, lifting the mattress and ripping pillows and opening cabinets and drawers and emptying jars of coffee and sugar and tossing folded clothes and towels and digging into every corner and cranny and then when he tried to open the closet it was locked. He banged the spike against the handle and the cheap door splintered and he yanked it open. The closet was thin and lined with shelves, stacks of Bibles and mason jars stuffed with cash and bottles of liquor and he raked them from the shelves, the bottles and jars knocking on the floor and the RV door flopped open with his movement and just as he snatched a cigar box from the top shelf, he heard the man in the doorway behind him.

'What the hell do you think you're doing?'

Holt ignored him. The cigar box was held shut with a small padlock. Holt dropped it on the floor and stomped it and the wooden box busted open and the thick keys rattled beneath the heel of his boot.

'I said what in the goddamn hell do you think you're doing?' the man said and he moved up the step of the RV and into the doorway.

Holt reached down and picked up the keys and then he charged the man, catching him offguard and the two barreled out of the doorway and crashed onto the pavement. Holt heard the slip of the knife from the overalls and he turned in time to draw back as it slashed before his eyes and Holt swung the spike and the man howled and dropped the knife, his nose exploding in red and Holt scrambled to his feet. He hustled to the camper door and reached in and snatched two jars of cash from the floor and when he turned and looked toward the revival, three of the workers were running toward him and he raced around the RV and out of the parking lot, making his way along the twisted route he had plotted out in the daylight, running through the ruins of roofless Main Street buildings and climbing up and over the crumbling brick wall of a church courtyard and finding the shadows of alleys and they could not keep up or keep track of Holt. He made it to the truck and opened the door and tossed the keys and jars and spike onto the bench seat as he climbed in. He cranked it and stomped the gas, bending into the road with tires squealing and in his rearview mirror he saw them come around the side of the building, heads shifting and looking for him. In only a moment he was away from the streetlights and when the road fell dark, a crack of lighting struck with such violence that he ducked and swerved off the road as if he was being shot at. And as he straightened the wheel and lifted his eyes, he wondered if the savage bolt was somehow speaking to him in a hardcrack of prophecy.

II

16

THE COYOTE EMERGED FROM THE blackwood and trotted across the clearing of the hillside, moving through the luminous night in the rangy gait of the under-fed. It crossed pastures and dipped beneath barbed wire fences and highstepped in the thick grass of forgotten fields as it hunted with a hanging tongue and sharp eyes. The starstruck night was filled with the symphony of crickets and frogs and whippoorwills and the coyote would stop to listen. Its black-tipped tail wagging and its ears raised. The predator's grin of bared teeth in the promise of the night.

It traveled on, moving from the emptiness of the hills and into the gatherings of hardwoods and pines where blueblack shadows fell across the forest floor. Inside the woods the coyote stopped to drink from a springfed creek that spilled from the earth in a silvery glide. The gangly animal lapped at the spring and then paused when a howl rose and fell in the distance and then the coyote raised its eyes to the moon in some nocturnal reverence before drinking again and moving on.

At the edge of an embankment it shuffled down carefully, slipping once and catching its balance and then coming out of the woods and moving along a fence row. The fence was wooden and slats were rotted and fallen and the coyote stepped through an opening and stood and peered into the roadside ditch where the weeds shifted with the movement of a small creature. The high moon a spotlight for the kill.

The coyote closed carefully. Front paws into the ditch. Tracking the movement. Hind legs then stepping in. The prey moved unaware as the coyote crept closer but then the coyote raised its head and looked down the road and toward the hum of the engine as the headlights appeared on the rim of darkness in the mechanical intrusion of nature's way.

17

O RON FELDER STOOD IN HIS backyard in unlaced
workboots and boxer shorts and a t-shirt. The night air
chilled the old man's arms and legs as he listened to the wail
of the coyote. Above him a wide open sky and a legion of
stars. The moonglow sank into the low fields that stretched
out from his small house on the small hill and the cool wind
blew through the staggered hardwoods.

He ran his hand across the top of his grayblack hair.
Scratched at his silvered beard. He could not help but be
curious about the coyote as it was something different tonight.
Not the yip yip yipping that was always there in the distance.
Tonight its voice was solitary. Something like pain. A final
effort to be heard across the night in these lands where it had
hunted and fought and defended its place with snarls and
fangs and blood. The old man imagined the coyote to be hurt
or injured in a way that it could not recover from and with
each winding wail in the dark the coyote's strength seemed
to diminish. Oron watched the sky for shooting stars and
listened to the animal and soon enough the howl was little
more than the cry of a helpless newborn and not that of a
clawed and seasoned predator.

Each night he stood in this spot in the backyard and found
comfort in the dark heavens. A ritual that helped him sleep.

He had outlived two wives and three sisters and a brother. A dozen cousins. Anybody worth a shit whose name he could remember. The last thing his son had said to him before he loaded up his family and headed for dryer ground was if you won't go with us at least promise me you won't be trying to get on and off your tractor anymore. You're eightythree years old and you ain't what you used to be.

I know how old I am.

The coyote cried and the old man licked the tip of his index finger and made a checkmark on the invisible scoreboard of life, adding the coyote to the total sum of who and what had gone before him and underneath the great sky the sense of being alone and injured in the depths of night settled inside him. The coyote howled again and this time the old man answered with his own aged and gravelly howl.

He went back inside and pulled on his trousers and a longsleeve shirt and then he picked up a straw fedora from the dresser. He walked back into the night and climbed into his truck and set off to look for the coyote. An uneven road trailed through his property and he followed it between the soggy fields, the headlights shining on the leaning fenceposts and barbed wire. The window was down and Oron leaned his head out and listened. Hearing the cry and moving along in its direction. It was a quartermile from his house to where the dirt met the asphalt of the county road and when he could see his mailbox he stopped. Killed the ignition.

He took off his hat and set it on the dashboard. Turned off the headlights. When it was quiet for too long he got out of the truck. No sound but the wind in the starbright world.

Maybe it's dead, he thought. Maybe we're all dead and just don't know it.

The coyote howled. The cry was coming from somewhere out along the road and he cranked the truck and eased to the end of his property and then he turned to the right, knowing it was close. He switched the headlights to highbeam and crept along and then he saw the eyes. Two bright dots peering at him from the ditch. The eyes of a killer. He parked and dimmed the headlights. Watched the eyes as they watched him. And then the coyote moved. It rose from the ditch and crossed the road and Oron had been right. Its hind leg dragged behind and its back haunch was smeared with blood and before it reached the other side of the road the coyote collapsed onto its side with a sorrowful whine.

He got out and walked toward the wounded animal, stopping several steps away. Aware of what it could still do. But the coyote seemed to be out of tricks. Wheezing and panting and every now and then a whimper. Beneath its backside the blood had made a little black pool.

He walked back to his truck and reached underneath the seat. He pulled out his pistol and returned to the coyote. The coyote's tongue fell out of its mouth and it turned its head just enough to put its eyes on Oron.

He clicked off the safety. Raised the pistol and slid his finger around the trigger and he was an instant from shooting when a shot from another gun gave a boom and the echo rolled across the empty night. Oron whipped his head around and ducked in the road. His old man knees hurting as he held still. A quiet moment passed as the echo faded and then there was another blast. Had to be a shotgun, he thought. From the opposite direction. A hundred yards away. He hurried to the truck and killed the headlights and stood there in the dark. The huffs and wheezes from the coyote. Hold on, he whispered to it. Hold on.

He looked back down the road in the direction of the blast and far into the black he noticed the red taillights pointed up in the ditch. He knew then that if he could see the road there would be skid marks, the moment when the vehicle saw the coyote and swerved to miss the coyote but hit it anyway and lost control. He also knew people upended in a ditch didn't fire shotguns. Not normal people.

The coyote had gone silent. The old man walked over to it and knelt beside the animal. He reached down and touched the coyote's ear and whispered to it. I know you feel better. Then he raised his eyes toward the taillights. And a figure passed in the red glow, crawling out of the ditch. Crawling into the road. Collapsing facedown.

The old man stood. He moved to the truck and set the pistol on the hood. He had always liked being outside in the night. Listening to the things that called and cried and moved. Something about the great reverence of an open sky made him think the world itself was in slumber. At peace for a few hours. That there were not such things as shotguns and people with their own reasons to fire them in the middle of damn nowhere. He picked up the pistol and reasoned with himself. If this is what it is, then this is what it is. And he began walking toward the headlights.

18

THE VEHICLE WAS A VAN. No plates. The windows of the back doors covered in tin foil. The rear tires were raised inches off the ground as the nose of the van stuck down into the earth, the headlights blotted out by mud and brush. The man who had crawled out lay facedown in the road. Breathing in staggered chunks. Frayed duct tape around his wrists and around his ankles that looked like it had been cut with something dull or maybe chewed. Oron stepped around him. Looking for the shotgun. And he found it lying in the roadside weeds. He picked it up and checked the chamber and it was empty. He had a flashlight in his truck and wished like hell he had it but did not want to move away now. Believing if he turned his back on this scene that the scene may come for him.

The passenger door of the van was open and Oron approached it with his pistol raised. A body lay against the dashboard with blood and brain sprayed on the busted windshield. He looked past the body to the driver's side expecting to see the same but the seat was empty and the door was open. Oron stepped back. Listened. He then moved back toward the road. Slowly. Trying not to make a sound.

He told himself to go home and call the damn law. Right now. The body in the road shifted. Grunted. Oron held the pistol pointed and the shotgun tucked under his arm and he was backing away from it all as another figure emerged from the other side of the van. Bent over and spitting blood and then as he fell to his knees a phone dropped from his hand, bouncing on the asphalt. The screen a small dot of light. A voice on the other end screaming some hostile question. The man dropped to all fours, spitting and bleeding and babbling in some language Oron had never heard, raising his head in the strange verbiage of a final conversation, calling out to the other side for help or mercy or maybe in horror of what he saw waiting there across the threshold. Oron stepped back as the man began to crawl and he talked and spit and then began to cry and that was the last sound he made before he fell faceflat and motionless.

Only one of them alive now. Oron walked a cautious circle around the man groaning in the middle of the road and then he moved to the van. He opened the back doors and the van was dark inside and he leaned the shotgun against the bumper and he took a lighter from his pocket and flicked it. He held the small flame out in front as he peeked into the van. A bench lined each wall and piles of clothes and shoes were scattered across the floor. A musty smell inside. Oron set the pistol down and picked through the clothes. Some for adults and some for children. Some for very small children. The man in the road groaned again and Oron turned surprised, almost forgetting he was there as the bodies missing from the clothes ran in naked and panicked circles in his mind. He picked up the pistol and slammed the van doors and the man had made it to his knees, trying to get to his feet.

'I'm calling an ambulance,' Oron said. 'Lay back down.'

'Don't,' the man said.

'I got to.'

'They'll kill us.'

'They're dead.'

The man coughed. Spit.

'Not them. The others.'

'There ain't no others. Lay down, boy. You're hurt.'

But he wouldn't lie down. He was pulling at the duct tape on his wrists. Touching the wallop on the side of his head. He moved on his knees to the van and put his hands on the bumper to help him to his feet and he managed to stand and he leaned against the vehicle, breathing hard and grimacing.

'I don't give a shit what you say,' Oron said. 'I'm going to call somebody.'

He turned and started walking for the truck, taking the shotgun. He ignored the man calling for him. Don't do it. Don't do it. Then came heaves and coughs and as Oron turned and looked the man was back to the ground. But Oron didn't stop. His mind was made up. He made it to his truck and set the shotgun and pistol on the seat and he cranked up. The headlights shined on the injured man and the dead man and the van and the whole awful mess and he was about to turn onto his property when new headlights appeared in the distance. The injured man saw them at the same time and he began to crawl for the ditch. Trying to get hidden. Getting flat on his stomach and trying to sink into the earth and Oron saw the duct tape around his ankles as he slunk down into the ditch and he knew the man was not in the van because he wanted to be and he had seen the clothes and shoes and God knows how many more had been in the back of the van who didn't want to be and the old man hit the brakes.

He got out and crossed the road and told the man to come on. Hurry. He held out his hand and the injured man took it and he pulled him from the ditch. He helped the man across the road and into the truck cab and then he stomped the gas, spinning tires and slinging mud as he turned onto his property. Slamming to a stop and getting out and closing the gate between the fenceposts and wrapping the chain around it though he had no lock but he did it anyway. He hopped back in the truck and killed the lights and shifted into drive. He let off the gas and the truck rolled, guided by the moonlight. He kept his eyes in the rearview mirror, waiting for the gate to swing open and hell to come on through.

19

JESSIE WOKE IN A SHOUT. Something faceless and foul reaching for her in her dreams. She sat up in the bed. Startled. Eyes darting in the dark. Confused as to where she was and what she was doing here and the moonshine fell into the room through the thin curtains and the dull light returned her to the nightmare. She had been living in a perpetual state of grab your shit and run until she finally had to grab her shit and run and her dreams mirrored her harried state. The hands reaching for her and reaching for Jace, the hands of gray figures that surrounded her in a blurred landscape where the wind howled and swirled and every direction was the wrong direction. She felt for the boy and found his chest and then his head. His soft hair. He slept on his back and she stroked his forehead with her thumb until it calmed her and then her eyes adjusted to the dark and she saw the frames on the wall. Her own childhood image staring back at her.

There was a bump in the hallway and she sat still. Held her breath. The movement came closer and then as the bedroom door pushed open she made fists. The head slid between the door and the frame and she was readying to yell some threat when instead the voice came tranquil and caring.

'Jessie,' Wade whispered.

She didn't answer.

'Jessie,' Wade said again. 'Are you all right?'

She sniffed. Unclenched her fists.

'Yes,' she whispered. 'I'm all right.'

'Are you sure?'

'Yes.'

'And the boy?'

'We're all right.'

Wade moved back out of the room and he closed the door. Jace smacked his lips in his sleep and rolled over on his side. She adjusted the blanket and covered him and then she lay back down and listened as a chair knocked on the hardwood floor in the kitchen and she knew her father had not been asleep but was instead awake. Watching and listening.

20

ORON DID NOT WANT TO turn on any house lights so he took a kerosene lamp from the mantel and struck a match and lit it and they sat there together in the amber light. The man sat on his rear and leaned in the open doorway. Oron sat across the room in a wooden chair that creaked with the slightest shift and he watched over the man's head for any spot of light or movement shifting in the black rectangle of the outerworld.

Oron studied the man. His hunched back and shoulders slumped forward as if being drawn back into the dark by the nightwind. Across the back of his neck the skin was rubbery and weblike. Scarred. The shiny skin ran across his neck and slipped down his back and disappeared underneath his shirt.

'You hurt?' the old man asked.

He nodded.

'Something broken?'

'Not that I know.'

'You bleeding from somewhere I can't see?'

'Not bad enough to look.'

The man was bruised and cut. Dirty hair and face. He wore a filthy flannel shirt that was ripped and bloodstained. He only wore one shoe. And it was big and clumsy and didn't seem to fit. He looked hungry. Oron was thinking of what else to ask him when his shoulder slid from the doorframe and he collapsed on his side and fell asleep.

Oron would have thought he was dead but for the immediate snore and deep breaths of exhaustion. The old man stood from the chair and eased across the room. Wondering if it was an act. An ambush disguised as dropdead sleep. Steps away he stopped and stared down at the man. Heaving from an open mouth. Slack arms and hands. Oron stepped over him and across the threshold. He sat down in an aluminum chair on the front porch. Staring down the road and toward the gate. The shotgun at his feet and the pistol in his lap.

His son called him every few weeks and told him to come and live with them. No, he answered every time. Why would I want to do that? Why wouldn't you? Do you want to be the last man standing? It is time to get out of there. Sell the land and the house. I couldn't get nothing for it, he answered. Not no more. You don't need the money anyway. Just come and live with us. You can have the room over the garage. Room over the garage, Oron had thought. Go and die over some garage in some neighborhood in some town. We won't bother you, his son told him. You can do what you want to do. I'm doing what I want to do now, he answered. And nobody bothers me. Not yet, his son said. I've heard stories. I watch the news. I know what's going on down there. It's just a matter of time.

The old man wanted to comfort his son in some way, let him know he was all right. That nobody was going to come knocking. But he couldn't tell him that. He didn't believe it himself. And now it felt as if he had been waiting for this very night for his entire life. He had been waiting for the man with the scars. Waiting for a van to nosedive in the ditch along the highway. Waiting for a coyote to give dying cries in the night.

The man on the floor let out a heavy snore and Oron turned and looked at him. The kerosene lamplight brushing his slumber. Then he looked back across the night. He expected to finally see the red and blue flashes of patrol cars and ambulances that would have come up on the wreck and found the bodies. A wrecker arriving to drag the van from the ditch. The voices and machines of rescue and recovery. But none of that happened. He stood from the chair and moved across the porch. The pistol tucked into the front of his pants.

I ain't scared of this. His eyes seemed to widen as the thought crossed his mind. I ain't scared of none of this shit. I have loved some good women. Plenty of good women come to think of it. And I drank plenty of good whiskey and I still can and I could grow tomatoes as big as a damm softball before all this damn weather. I ain't scared of no storm and I've fished people out of floods and off rooftops with nothing but a damn fishing boat and troller motor. I raised a boy into a man and I did my best to keep promises to people and I ain't hardly blinked at the bad news that won't stop coming and I ain't scared of none of this shit. Eightythree years old and I'll ride my damn tractor if I want to ride it. I'll ride it all the way to New Orleans. Right down the middle of the Quarter and I'll park it and drink a damn beer and find me a damn woman if I want to. I shot a damn nail right through my hand with a nail gun and pulled the son of a bitch out myself and wrapped my hand up in a sock and finished the damn day and didn't make a damn whimper and I took a beating every time the damn market crashed and I ain't missed a meal yet and nobody in my family missed a damn meal. I ain't living in no room above no damn garage and I ain't scared of this night or the next night or the night after. I don't give a shit what happens.

Come on. Whatever you are. Just come on.

21

WADE HAD ALWAYS TOLD HIMSELF he was trying. That helped somehow. It had been easier when she was small. It was easier to answer her questions and appease her. It was easier to watch her grow and learn and run and play and sing and dance and be exactly what he thought she would be. But then she began to turn into something different. Something more than just a little girl. And it became apparent to him that he wasn't going to be everything she needed and that's when they both began to hurt a little worse for Rebecca. Jessie turned thirteen and then fourteen and it got a little worse. She talked less when they were riding in the truck or eating dinner. A bedroom door closed between them more often during the waking hours. Her coming and going with friends that he knew and didn't know and when she was out he began to step into her room and look around, never brave enough to open any drawers or push back clothes and look into closet corners but he would move about the room with eyes on whatever lay on the floor or on the nightstand. Her As and Bs turned into Cs and sometimes Ds and he grounded her for it and she yelled at him for it and somewhere in there he decided the best thing to do was to get out of the damn way.

He was in demand working the big rigs that tended the soybean and corn crops across south Mississippi and down into

Louisiana and in the time in between harvests he decided to go offshore, working a crane on a platform somewhere out in the Gulf of Mexico. Gone for two weeks at a time. Leaving Jessie to sleep on the couches of relatives or stay over with friends while he was away. And while he was away she had begun to make her own rules. She had begun to turn into a young woman. During the two weeks Wade was at home she came and went as she pleased and whenever they talked it was him trying to figure out what she was doing and who she was doing it with and she wasn't interested in anything he had to say and they talked less and less and he drank more and more. Somewhere in there she got a driver's license and her friends had theirs and father and daughter turned into strangers passing one another in the kitchen or outside the house. He had always told himself he was trying but even then there was a whisper just below that said you are not trying and you know it and she is slipping away. But it was only a whisper and it could be washed down with a bottle at any given moment.

Jessie kept evolving and then one day a man showed up. Not a boy. Not some lanky little harddick high school boy with mudflaps on his truck but a man. A dozen years older than Jessie. A man who pulled up in front of the house and let down his tailgate and sat on it and smoked and waited for Jessie to come out. Never honking the horn. Never coming up on the porch and knocking on the door. Just sitting there waiting for her to come out and go with him.

Wade had watched him through the living room window. Sitting there. Hard shoulders and a hard brow and tight eyes as he drew on the cigarette. Who the hell is that, he asked her. Why do you care, she said. Because you're seventeen goddamn years old that's why. And he ain't nowhere close to that. You don't give a shit, she said. And this was their conversation over and over until Wade finally met him in the yard and told him you got a lot of fucking nerve pulling up to my house and not even having the manners to walk up to the door and knock or speak to the father of the girl you're sniffing around and she's too young for you anyhow but I figure you know that and don't give a shit. Chicken shit. Get in that piece of shit truck and turn around and don't bother coming back. The man only smoked and looked past Wade toward the house. You hear me? Wade said. But he only smoked and looked past him until Jessie came out and then there was more shouting between Wade and Jessie and then shouting and shoving as he grabbed her by the arm and told her she wasn't going anyfuckingwhere and then they wrestled and she got away and told him to go to hell and she got in the truck and they drove off. This man never saying a word or raising a finger as Wade and Jessie went at it.

A month later she turned eighteen and she was gone.

He thought of that day now as he sat at the kitchen table. A silent night. A glass of water on the table that he turned and turned as he remembered pulling at her, trying to force her back into a life she wanted no part of. He had always told himself that he tried but he didn't believe it.

He got up from the table and moved silently across the room. He opened the front door and stepped out onto the porch and he looked out at the driveway that led from the slope of the yard and split the sagging acres of cornstalks and he pretended to see headlights coming in the distance. The vehicle moved closer and stopped in the yard and then he watched himself get out of the car and hurry around to the other side and open the door for Rebecca. He helped her out of the car as she held the tiny wrapped bundle. She moved gingerly and he held her elbow as they crossed the yard and he was smiling and she was smiling and his mind was filled with what the coming years would have been like with picnics and birthday parties and anniversaries and all the mundane shit that people walk right past. But nothing had been mundane and he had made it worse for Jessie and he goddamn knew it, staring out into the night and this great gnawing that chewed on his insides. He had told himself he was trying and he had always known it was bullshit but there was a greater potency in his regret now as she lay in the other room. A grown woman with a child of her own and nothing better to do than to run back home to him.

He went back inside and he heard her shout. He went to the bedroom to check on her and when she said she was okay he returned to the kitchen table and sat down again. She wakes up from bad dreams, he thought. Her father's child.

22

HOLT SAT UP ON THE floor. The old man had fallen asleep in the aluminum chair with the shotgun propped against his leg. Holt lay back down and stretched out and formed an X. The light from the kerosene lamp wobbled against the ceiling and a chorus of frogs sang beneath the stardipped sky. Oron shifted in the rocker and the shotgun fell and banged against the porchboards and both of them sat up straight, expecting someone to be there but there was only the same scene that they had shared through the night.

Oron reached down and grabbed the shotgun barrel. Holt grunted and rose to his feet. He crossed the porch and sat down on the steps. He then peeled off the filthy shirt and the scars that started on his neck stretched down his back and reached to his waistline.

'You seen anything?' he asked Oron.

'No. Nothing.'

'You hear anything?'

'Ain't heard nothing. Ain't seen nothing. Maybe you're a ghost. Maybe it was all pretend.'

Holt looked back at Oron.

'Are you worried?' he asked.

'About what?'

'About what you see.'

'I told you. I ain't seen nothing.'

Oron studied the scarred skin of Holt's back and shoulders. Holt noticed the dark and wrinkled skin of the old man. Time marking them both in its own brotherly way.

A long pause fell between them. Something howled. Holt turned his eyes back toward the night.

'Who were they?' Oron asked.

'There's more of them.'

'I figured that.'

'They're looking for something.'

'And I guess you have it,' Oron said.

'Maybe.'

'You either have it or you don't.'

'I don't have it but maybe I know where it is. Maybe.'

Oron stood from the aluminum chair. He carried the pistol and shotgun with him as he walked into his bedroom. He took a sweatshirt and pair of socks from an armoire and an old pair of boots from the back of the closet and he returned to the porch and dropped it all next to Holt. He picked up the sweatshirt and pulled it over his head.

'Don't know what size you are but maybe those boots will wear.'

Holt removed his one shoe and tossed it out into the yard. Then he pulled on the socks and tried to pull on the boots but they were too small. He set them aside and said thanks anyway.

'You sure you don't need me to take you to a hospital or something?'

'Where am I?' Holt asked.

'My house.'

'On the map.'

'Straddling Mississippi and Louisiana.'

97

'Which side?'

'Mississippi side.'

'Are they gone?'

'I don't know,' Oron said. 'I told you I didn't hear nothing or see nothing and then I nodded off.'

'How long was I out on the floor?'

'Not that long. Hour or two.'

'How long were you out in the chair?'

'About a minute.'

'You didn't go out there and check?'

'Check what?'

'To see if anybody was out there.'

'They ain't my business.'

'I wish that was true.'

'What does that mean?'

'You see me don't you?' Holt said.

'I see you.'

'Then it don't matter if you think they are your business or not. They are.'

Oron sat forward and he realized he could put the pistol behind the man's ear and pull the trigger and this would be the end of whatever had begun. No matter if this man was the good guy or the bad guy or somewhere in between he could have this all done by daybreak with a bullet and a shovel and then life could be what it was when the sun last came up. It was a wild thought but it felt like possibility in the ransacked rules of the hurricane South. Holt turned and looked at him as if reading the old man's mind and it caught Oron offguard. He slid his finger around the pistol trigger.

The old man then stood from the aluminum chair and for reasons he did not understand he laid the shotgun across the chairseat and set the pistol on the porch rail and he moved down the steps and he stood in the yard. He expected to hear the click of the shotgun and he expected to hear the blast and then the angels singing glory hallelujah but he only heard the man on his porch cough and then spit. He turned and faced him.

'What you want from me?'

'You're the one who brought me here,' Holt said. 'How do you know I didn't want to stay right where I was?'

'I could sure as hell drag your ass back out there.'

He knew the man did not put himself into the van but Oron wondered now if he had somehow deserved to be there. But then he remembered the piles of clothes and shoes in the back of the van and the rank and dour smell that spilled out of the doors and he did not believe anyone deserved to be there. The van a vessel of nightmares. How many dozens or hundreds or maybe thousands had sat in the back of the van helpless and hungry and scared and wondering how there could be such a life.

A screech crossed the land.

The old man walked a circle. Kicked at the discarded shoe. Then he asked Holt again what it was he wanted because the sun will rise and things will look and feel different and I'm guessing neither one of us will be as brave in the light of day. But Holt did not answer. He had laid back on the porch and collapsed again into sleep.

Life is long, Oron thought. It was the recollection of an idea from a book or the line in some old movie. And he imagined himself as a boy roughhousing it with another kid outside a church and then he saw himself as a teenager with his head jerking as he learned how to drive a stickshift and he kept recalling the memories that stretched back decades. The lengthy blues and purples of dusk. The hours spent drinking beer and smelling the meat that was cooking on a grill. Watching children. Being alone. Life is long, he thought again. He wondered if the man on the floor would ever have such revelations or if he already had them while he was locked inside the van.

The old man's thoughts were interrupted by a vehicle maybe a mile or more in the distance. Something noisy and incapable of surprise. The vehicle roared but then slowed and its sound lessened. The engine idled for a long moment and then turned off. The thud of closing doors. Oron began to walk along the gravel driveway and headlights shined along the highway in the direction of his property. He crept along with the dark holding him and when the voices grew louder he paused. Shouts of anger and frustration. His curiosity had started him walking with neither the pistol nor the shotgun and his vulnerability hit him as he wondered what he would do if the headlights turned into his driveway and what if a reckless vehicle bashed through the gate and what if it sped toward him and what if they came with guns blazing or what if they wanted to throw him into the back of a van and that's when he heard the engine roar and he was caught in the beams but it was not coming from the road but from behind him, his own truck racing from the house and toward him and he dove out of the way and into the grass. He tumbled but raised his head in time to see his truck crash through the gate, the tires squealing as it leaned hard onto the highway and then slammed to a stop. Gunshots all at once. Blistering echoes and white flashes and glass shattering and more screams and shouts and then there was nothing.

Oron listened. Only the hum of his own truck engine remained.

He got to his feet and sneaked along the driveway. The gruffsounding vehicle cranked and then another shotgun blast. He stopped. Waited for another blast or for groans and moans but the gruffsounding engine was cut off again. He recognized the shift of his own truck and heard the engine rise and fall and knew the truck was moving backward and then forward and then his own headlights appeared at the end of the driveway, two hotwhite eyes coming toward him and the old man turned and ran, looking back over his shoulder and into the approaching beams and his gait awkward and aged and the truck came on him and he had begun to cry as he ran toward what could only be the end of it all and he thought life is short and hell yes I'm scared and then he tripped and fell and raised his head and looked back in time to watch the truck slam the brakes and slide to a stop only an arm's length from the old man's tearstreaked face.

Dust and bugs danced in the beams. Oron felt the heat of the engine on his face through the front grille. He fell back from his knees and sat there in the gravel and waited. A voice called from the open window.

'Get up and get in,' Holt said.

Oron didn't move. Couldn't move. This night emptying him and it wasn't over yet.

'I said get up and get in. They're gonna come here and you don't want to be here when they do.'

Oron leaned forward and grabbed the bumper of his truck. Pulled and lifted himself to his knees and then his feet. He glared into the shadowed cab and wiped his eyes with the back of his hand.

'I ain't going nowhere with you,' Oron said. 'And get your ass out of my truck.'

'If you don't think that mess out there is gonna cross the road to your place then you're a fool.'

'I don't care. I'll be a fool.'

'I'm trying to help you.'

'I don't need no help. Get out of my goddamn truck.'

The truck idled. The two men stared at one another. Across the land the first shades of blue stroked the eastern horizon.

'Last chance,' Holt said. 'Get in or get left.'

Oron did not answer. The engine revved. The pistol was flung from the window and bounced in the gravel. The old man stood motionless as the truck shifted into reverse and eased away, backing all the way down the driveway. The headlights shrinking in goodbye.

23

ORON PICKED UP THE PISTOL and he went into the barn and pulled the cover off the old Buick. It had been his second wife's car before she died and he had kept it and drove it every few weeks to keep it running. Nearly thirty years since they had gone to Jackson and driven it off the lot but it had never been wrecked and seldom driven over sixty miles an hour and now it was his vessel into a new world.

He left the barn and returned to the house. He went into the bedroom and pulled a suitcase from the closet and he began to toss clothes into it without regard. A sloppy pile of shirts and pants and underwear that he pressed down to be able to close the suitcase and he carried it with him into the living room and set it on the floor. He returned the kerosene lamp to the mantel and in the tawny light he looked around at the relics of a life. As if he was now the intruder. And he wondered if and when the bad men came to his place if they would destroy the frames and the furniture and burn it all down or if they would sit in the comfortable chairs with their guns resting on their knees and try to figure out what to do next.

He picked up the suitcase and closed the door behind him. He didn't bother to lock it. He stopped in the yard and set the suitcase on the dewdrenched grass. The stars had begun to flake away in the first light.

He heard them coming along the highway. One engine sound and then a louder one. They turned onto his road and the two vehicles soon parked side by side. Doors opened and men got out and a handful of them stood in front of the headlights, their bodies and the weapons they held in silhouette.

'Where is he?' a voice called.

Oron did not answer.

'Hey. Old man. Where the hell is he? We saw your tracks in the road. We know you went looking around.'

Oron touched the handle of the pistol tucked into his pants and as if called to arms all the men raised their weapons and leveled them on the old man. And they began to spread, small steps of separation as they stalked and formed a corral around him and the voice kept shouting threats and commands and Oron held his hand on the pistol but as they closed on him he did not look at the bad men and he did not listen to whatever was being shouted in his direction. His focus was on this place around him. His hills and his fences and his barn that he raised himself when he was a much younger man. The road he went up and down every day working his ass off and paying bills and maneuvering the obstacles of life to arrive at this moment. He ran his eyes around the rim of the sky where he had watched the sun rise in the mornings in a golden hue and set in the evenings in a bloodorange strip of melancholy. Only a sprinkle of stars remained and he stared at them and the men closed around him but he admired the tiny lights of worlds unknown and in those stars he now felt peaceful and fearless. The threats and the guns were paid no attention at all. It was as if he stood alone.

I ain't scared of none of this shit, he thought.

And it was the last thought that passed through his mind as he raised the pistol to his temple and fired.

24

HOLT DROVE THE TRUCK HARD and fast, leaving the old man standing in his yard and the mess of wreckage and bodies on the side of the road and wary of any vehicles that approached on the empty highway. He drove until he felt safe enough and when he saw an open gate he pulled off the road, the truck rattling as it crossed a cattle gap and he shut the headlights and shut the ignition and sat mute and still in the embrace of dawn.

He rubbed his wrists where the duct tape had bound him. He touched the various bruises and knots that came with the fists and knees that were delivered when he wouldn't tell them what they wanted to hear. He smelled himself and he stunk. A growl rose from his stomach and he could not remember the last thing he had eaten. He let his head drop against the steering wheel and then he collapsed and his body flopped over in the seat like the dead.

III

25

MORNING. THE WOLF SAT ON its haunches and with bluewhite eyes it stared at the man in coveralls and the two women. One of the women held a Coke can and the other held a cigarette.

'I'm telling you. She was holding a kid and she came right out of the woods,' said the woman with the Coke.

'What was she doing out there in the woods?' the other said.

'I don't know.'

'Sounds made up.'

'Why the hell would I make it up?'

'Y'all both shut it,' the man in coveralls said. 'Don't matter if she was carrying a kid or a goshdang raccoon she ain't here and neither is the cold dead body we're supposed to be showing to Elser.'

At the mention of her name the three went quiet. The women looked at the ground. The man looked over at the wolf who was waiting to be fed.

'You think she can really do it?' said the woman with the cigarette.

'Do what?'

'You know what. See stuff.'

'If she could see stuff then why don't she know where this

fellow is we're supposed to be helping her track down?' the man said.

'It don't work like that.'

'Then how does it work?'

'I can't say exactly but I seen it happen.'

The others waited on the woman to finish her thought but she had to first finish the cigarette. She took a final draw and then flicked it away and went on with her story.

'I went to one of her shows one time and saw her tell some old man exactly what day he was going to die and sure enough the son of a bitch died the very day she predicted.'

'Bullshit,' the man said.

'I heard that same thing,' the other woman said.

'Y'all are both crazy as Elser.'

'She ain't crazy.'

'I ain't playing,' the woman said. 'He was sitting on the back row with his arms folded as if he didn't believe none of what was going on and she picked him out. Called him right down to the altar and told him he better get his shit straight. Better get down on his knees and ask for all his sins to be flushed and apologize to the Lord and to everybody he knew for anything bad he'd ever done because he was going to be visiting the gates in about three days. Three days later he fell out dead behind the wheel of his car and ran right off into the swamp and sunk to the bottom.'

'Says who?' the man said.

'Says everydamnbody in that town.'

'What town?'

'I can't recall.'

'She can do it,' the other woman agreed and she tossed the Coke can on the ground. 'It's just got to hit her right. That's what I heard.'

'I don't know what she can do when it comes to seeing shit or healing the sick or calming the raging sea but I do know we better have a good goshdang excuse for why what she told us to do ain't been done.'

'It was done. Kinda.'

'Like I said,' the man said. 'We better have a good excuse.'

'Yeah. We better.'

'It's the woman from the woods. It's her fault.'

'See how that works,' the man said. 'I don't know how to explain none of it. Unless one of you is lying.'

The wolf rose from its haunches and began to pace. Whining and hungry. The heavy chain dragging the smooth ground where the wolf lived its life.

The women looked at each other.

'I ain't lying,' one of them said.

'I sure as hell ain't.'

'Because if either one of y'all found the keys on him and are keeping a little secret then you know it won't end like you think it's gonna end,' he said.

'How do we know you ain't the one lying?'

'Yeah. How do we know you didn't find the keys and is standing here lying about it? Talking all big and bad.'

'Shut it,' he said.

'You shut it.'

The sound of the approaching hearse echoed across the empty land.

'Let me do the talking,' he said.

'I figure she'll let talk who she wants to let talk,' the other woman said.

'Yeah,' he said. 'That sounds about right.'

Almost simultaneously they all took out cigarettes and lit

them. A trio of anxiety as the roughrunning engine chugged closer.

'You really think she can see stuff?' the man said.

Both women nodded.

The hearse rolled to a stop next to a barrel of burning trash. It was coated in layers of dust and grime and bore the shape of some mechanical mercenary.

'Shit,' one of the women said.

Elser got out.

Her cheeks seemed drawn in some perpetual inhale and the lines around her eyes and forehead were defined and angular like streaks of lightning. Her nose was pointed and a fraction offcenter and her gaze felt distant even in close proximity. As if she didn't really believe you were there. She began to pace around the plot, not looking at any of them but instead taking in the wolf and piles of bricks and old tires and the smoke rising from the barrel. None spoke. They only watched and waited until she turned toward them.

'You've gotten fatter,' she said to the man in coveralls.

The two women grinned at one another.

'So have you,' she said to them. 'Maybe instead of sitting around eating you could all put your heads together and figure out how to do what the hell I asked you to do.'

They all nodded.

'Speak goddamn it.'

'Yes ma'am,' they said.

Elser rubbed her forehead. She looked around again.

'So. Where is he?'

'Well,' the man in coveralls said. 'He's gone.'

'What does that mean?'

'It means he ain't here no more,' one of the women said.

'I know what gone means. What I don't know is how a dead man can no longer be in the place you said he was in.'

'You won't believe it,' the man said.

'Tell me anyway.'

'We came out this morning and wrapped him up and stuck him in the back of the car. And then we were waiting on you before we took him off and buried him. Just like you said. But then this woman came out of the woods.'

He paused then. Waiting on Elser's reaction. When there wasn't one he kept going.

'I was getting coffee back inside and heard this commotion. The wolf jumping and them two yelling and I run out and there was this woman carrying this youngun. Came right out of the woods over there. She ran over and got in the car and hightailed it out of here. We tried to stop her.'

Elser folded her arms. Dropped her head in disgust or disbelief or both.

'They were supposed to be watching,' the man said.

'Liar,' one of the women said.

'We were watching,' the other said.

'I guess not.'

'Neither was you.'

'Hush,' Elser said, her head rising in a snap. 'Just hush. All of you.'

She walked a small circle then looked at the man.

'A woman ran out of the woods. With a baby.'

'More like a toddler.'

'A woman ran out of the woods. With a toddler. Got in the car. Drove away. While the three of you sat here and watched.'

They nodded.

'And the man in the back of the car. It wasn't Holt.'

'No ma'am,' the man said.

'Did this other person have the keys?'

'No ma'am.'

'Why'd you kill him?'

'It was an accident.'

'An accident.'

'Yes ma'am.'

'Explain it to me.'

'We seen him at the gas station buying beer. He had some scars like you said. Right about the same age that you said. We started talking to him and figured he was lying and then we got into it and next thing you know we were out here wrapping him up and stuffing him in the back of the car.'

'So you don't know who he was.'

'He told us.'

'What'd he say?'

'He said I ain't the man you're looking for and I don't know nothing about no keys.'

'I meant what was his name?'

They all looked at one another. The women both shrugged.

'Do any of you have any idea how many people are looking for Holt?'

'A lot,' the man said.

'A lot. Do you really think Holt would tell you he was Holt or tell you he had the keys?'

'Probably not.'

'So do you see now why I needed to see the body? Or better yet talk to a live body?'

'Yes ma'am.'

'Because he was around here somewhere. We do know that. That's why we called you.'

'I know it,' the man said.

'You don't know shit and I wonder if you would know shit if it was smeared across your face. Why the hell didn't you chase her?'

The man pointed at the truck with the raised hood and missing tire.

Elser sighed. She held out her hand and one of the women gave her a cigarette. Elser pulled out a matchbox and lit it.

'I prayed for you,' she said. Not looking at them but instead looking over their heads and into the morning sky. 'I prayed for all of you this morning as I drove in your direction. The deeper we fall into sin the deeper the prayers must be. And the three of you are in deep. Where the fire burns like the sun.'

She smoked. Her eyes on the tufts of passing clouds.

A car appeared in the distance, emerging from a gathering of hardwoods along the blackdirt road. The eyes of the sinners rose to meet it.

'We didn't mean it,' the man said. 'We're sorry. Really sorry. We'll do better. I swear it.'

The women echoed his apologies and nodded in submission.

Elser waved her cigarette hand to hush them.

'This is not a call to the altar,' she said. Her eyes fell from the clouds and landed on the three of them. 'This is judgment.'

Elser was small and bony and the man in coveralls knew he could crush her and he gave a look to the two women and their eyes reflected his own fear as the car approached and Elser smoked and the wolf whined. He knew he could crush her but he also knew he could outrun the two women and he dashed away from them and in the direction that Jessie and Jace had sprung from the woods, running past the wolf but misjudging the chain and the wolf leapt and clamped its white fangs down on the man's forearm and the man screamed as he dropped to a knee and tried to yank free but the teeth had sunk into the skin and the red soaked his sleeve as the wolf snarled and tasted blood and the two women took off and ran right past him as he cried out for their help but their thick legs churned and their thick arms pumped as they disappeared into the trees just as the car pulled to a stop next to the hearse.

The tall man with the blackrimmed glasses sat behind the wheel but he did not get out. Three other men emerged from the vehicle and Elser pointed and gave directions and then she walked over to the car and she and the tall man spoke for a moment through the open window before she returned to the hearse. The three men had taken gas cans that sat beside the brokendown truck and were dousing the front doors and windows of the cabin and the trailer while the man in coveralls screamed in torment as the wolf would not relinquish its clamp on his forearm and when the men poured the gas on the man they thought the wolf would let go but it held on to its last meal and everything burned together.

26

JACE POKED HIS TINY FINGER into the chin of his sleeping grandfather. His head turned to the side and flat against the kitchen table and his mouth agape in an uncomfortable sleep. The boy poked him again and Wade's eyes opened.

'Milk,' the boy said.

Wade raised his head from the table, his face twisted in a grimace as he grabbed and rubbed at the crick in his neck. He moaned. Stood and stretched. Then he looked down at Jace.

'Milk,' the boy said again and he pointed at his mouth.

Jessie woke and saw that Jace wasn't in bed with her. She sat up and smelled coffee and heard Wade knocking around in the kitchen and asking Jace if he wanted a piece of bacon so she lay back down and listened to them. Jace's sweet voice saying yes or no when Wade asked him if he slept good or if he wanted the bacon to be more crispy or if he liked baseball. She barely recognized her father's voice as he talked to the boy. Patient and calm.

She rose from the bed and closed the bedroom door. She picked up her jacket from the floor and felt in the pocket and pulled out the keys. The big and clunky keys to a big and clunky lock. She ran her fingers across the hardness of the curves and cuts and she imagined that they unlocked thick doors in dingy dungeons where the people behind those doors were filthy and hungry and bound to the wall by rusted chains.

She looked across the room at her school photographs that hung in no particular pattern on the bedroom wall. I have Jace and the keys and the pistol and the clothes I'm wearing and that is the grand total. It seemed improbable to her, as if traipsing through the world bound and blindfolded could result in a better haul.

The first time she had seen Holt he was sitting on the tailgate of his truck and drinking a milkshake. She and her friends pulled up to the dairy bar and ordered hamburgers and fries. A late afternoon. Her hair tangled from riding with the windows down. While they waited her friends passed around a joint and Jessie returned to the car and looked for a brush. When she couldn't find one she called to her friends and asked for one but they all shrugged.

'I got one,' he said.

She looked at him. His hair was short and choppy as if he cut it himself.

'Then use it,' one of her friends said.

'Give it here then,' Jessie said.

He hopped off the tailgate and grabbed a brush from the glovebox and she met him halfway.

'You need it worse than me,' she said.

'Keep it.'

'She don't want that nasty brush,' one of her friends called.

'Shut up,' she called back.

When Holt turned to walk back to the tailgate she saw the scars across the back of his neck. She watched him until he sat down and then they watched each other and she stood in the space between him and her friends and she ran the brush through her tangled hair. When the woman at the dairy bar slid open the glass and held out the bags of burgers and fries, Jessie did not turn and join her friends at the picnic table at the side of the building but instead she went and sat on the tailgate beside Holt.

She dropped the heavy keys on the bed and lay back down. Eyes to the ceiling. It would have helped if she knew what the keys meant. What they unlocked. What chest or room they opened. But she did understand one important thing about them. People with bad intentions wanted them and those people were not afraid to spill blood.

Holt never said much and that was what she had liked about him. The silence they could share. Home was a battlefield. Wade's hard voice and her hard voice in routine hard collisions. Holt offered little and asked for little. Beneath a hardened brow his eyes were brittle, eyes that seemed to tell the story of the scars on his back and neck. Scars she never asked about. She never asked him why he was living in a motel or what he did for money. They were questions she was never sure she wanted the answers to. He was quiet and he was serious and he was lean and she could tell he had been in fights and lived hard and he smiled when she said something funny and he listened when she told him about her mother dying in childbirth. She never asked him about his own family and she wondered if his own family had something to do with the scars. She would meet him in the motel parking lot on Highway 51 and they would listen to the radio and smoke and then he started showing up in the senior parking lot behind the high school where she and her friends skipped class. When she asked him how old he was he said twentysomething and even that felt fine to her. She didn't need to know everything about him. She knew everything there was to know about everybody in the place she was born and raised and she wasn't interested in any of them.

And she hated to admit it then and she hated to admit it now but he reminded her of her father, the way Wade stared out at the land when he sat alone on the porch. The way sometimes at night he seemed genuinely incapable of speaking. Though the time had come and gone when she wanted Wade to come closer and even though she resented him she recognized and found strength in the look. She saw it when she looked at Wade and she saw it when she looked at Holt and she saw it when she looked in the mirror.

Holt hadn't told her about the keys until a week after she left home with him. They were at a campsite off the side of the interstate. A tent and a cooler their first purchases after they left Wade standing in the yard. A fire burned inside a circle of stones. He sat on the cooler and she sat on the ground pulling apart a pinecone and tossing it into the flames.

'People are looking for me,' he had said.

She laughed.

'By people you mean Wade.'

'No. Not that.'

'Who is looking for you?' she asked.

'I don't know exactly.'

'Then how do you know someone is?'

'It's more than one.'

'Huh?'

'It's not just one person. I don't even know how many but probably a lot.'

'What are you talking about?'

'I'm trying to tell you.'

She quit laughing.

'Why are these people looking for you?' she said.

'I got something and they want it.'

She stood up. Wiped her hands.

'Stop messing with me.'

'I'm not,' he said. 'And I won't.'

'That's exactly what it sounds like to me.'

He slowly took her hand and had her sit next to him on the cooler. He told her about it all. And the descriptions of Elser and the revival and the holy child and the tall man seemed outlandish and felt like a wellfashioned story to make himself sound interesting. Part of her wanted to stand back up and demand to be taken home. Then he told her about the map with notes drawn all over it and the keys and how he came to steal the keys and the men who beat the shit out of him but he managed to get away and the stronger part of her was exhilarated by the idea. Whether it was real or in his head.

'I saw them,' he said. 'The day before we left.'

'How do you know?'

'I just know. I can only stay in one place for so long and then I see them.'

'What do they look like?'

'Like they want to hurt you.'

'You're screwing with me.'

'I already told you I'm not.'

'Why didn't you tell me before?'

'I didn't see them before.'

'Where did you see them?'

'After I dropped you off at the house. A car pulled out of a driveway about a halfmile down the road where I never saw a car before. It followed me to the motel.'

'What'd you do?'

'I kept going. Drove back through town and made some turns to see if I was right and they kept following. I cut hard through some neighborhoods and alleys and lost them. Then I hid out all night parked off in the woods.'

'And the next day you told me you were leaving?'

He nodded.

'And you wanted me to go with you.'

He nodded again.

'And I told my dad to go to hell and here we sit.'

'They had seen you with me. I know it. You had to come with me.'

She had bent over and dropped her head between her knees and let out a big exhale. When she rose up she slapped at her own cheeks as if to wake herself from a dream.

'I didn't tell you before because I didn't want you to think I was crazy,' he said.

'Well.'

'I'm not crazy, Jessie.'

'You ain't sane either. Neither am I apparently. Christ almighty.'

She stood from the bed now and picked up the framed sunset photograph from Wade's dresser. She wished that leaving home could have been as simple as being mad at her father. She wished the story was as old as that. There had been so many days when she hated him and he did not understand her and she did not understand him and all she wanted to do was leave. She had been thirteen years old the first time she uttered the words fuck this place. Already imagining herself out of Pike County. Away from Mississippi. Maybe away from the country. Anywhere but here. She thought of those first days after she left. She thought now of Wade alone and she remembered the pride she felt in showing him what it felt like when he was offshore. She had never once called or mailed a letter or communicated in any way to let him know she was alive or okay or pregnant and now he was in the other room. And she had come home because she needed help. The last damn reason on earth she ever wanted to return.

Holt had told her twice in the last three years he would take her back. The first time they were shot at after a bar fight and they barely escaped and they sat huffing and puffing behind a dumpster waiting to make a run for it. The second time was when she told him she was pregnant. Both times she said no. I'm with you.

I'm still with you, she thought.

She wanted to go throw the keys in the woods and forget about it all. But they were far beyond that. She set the picture frame back on the dresser and pulled a rubberband from her wrist and put her dirty blonde hair in a ponytail. She opened the bedroom door to join them and she heard Wade tell Jace it would have been nice if your mother would have said something to me about you. Or about anything.

27

JACE WAS LYING ON HIS back on the couch with his feet up in the air. Jessie crossed the room and pinched his toes and he laughed and then he said hey momma. She picked him up and hugged him. Asked him if he had his milk or if he was hungry and he nodded and pointed at Wade.

'We got a little bacon and toast and not much else,' he said.

'I ain't hungry.'

'Do you drink coffee?'

'Yeah,' she said.

She set Jace down on the couch. Wade poured her a cup and she sat at the small round table and he picked up Jace's plate and cup and set them in the sink. Then he poured a refill and sat down with her. The morning sun fell slanted across the room and a heap of ashes smoldered in the fireplace. Wade nodded toward the window and said it looks like a nice day.

'You been out?' she asked.

'On the porch.'

'Still cold?'

'When the wind blows.'

She sipped. Jace tumbled from the couch and said ouch but then he climbed right back up.

'Go ahead,' Jessie said.

Wade didn't answer. She looked at him until he caught her eyes.

'I said go ahead.'

'I thought you were talking to him.'

'I wasn't.'

He stood and took a cigarette from a pack on the counter but he only held it between his fingers and he sat back down.

'What do you mean?' he said.

'Ask me. I know you're dying to.'

'I don't even know which question to pick.'

They would not look at each other now. Both watching the boy. Both drinking coffee.

'Does that television work?' she asked.

Wade nodded. He got up and turned it on and said I can't say I know where the cartoons are.

'Just pick something,' she said. 'He don't really care.'

Wade clicked until he came to a Western and he stopped.

'Horse,' Jace said and pointed.

Wade returned to the table with Jessie. He seemed stunted. Unable to process others being there with him.

'I ain't gonna offer again,' she said.

'Okay,' he said. 'Where you been and what you been doing and who you been doing it with?'

'That's three questions.'

'That's the very beginning.'

'I ain't giving you my life story.'

'You told me to ask.'

'A question. Not a hundred.'

On the television screen, pistols and rifles fired as cowboys dove behind water troughs and between the swinging doors of saloons and horses reared and yanked free from posts and fled.

She would not look at her father. She watched the boy watching the television and Wade ran his eyes along her thin neck and thin arms and there was a scar on the back of her hand he didn't recognize. He pulled a lighter from his pocket and flicked it and then set it on the table.

'Where is he?' he asked.

She shook her head.

'Is that his?' he said and he pointed at Jace.

Then she looked at Wade.

'That?'

'You know what I mean.'

'You mean your grandson.'

'Until this moment I can't say I thought of it that way.'

'That's what he is.'

'I know.'

'Then is my grandson his?'

'Yeah.'

'And you don't know where he is?'

She shook her head again.

Good, he thought. I hope the son of a bitch fell down a well somewhere. He got up and poured two glasses of water at the sink and returned to the table. He slid her a glass and she picked it up and drank. Her hand a little shaky. He picked up the cigarette and fiddled with it.

'You look like shit,' she said.

'I quit drinking. It's supposed to have the opposite effect.'

'Bullshit.'

'No. I did.'

'Why?'

'What?'

'Why did you quit drinking?'

'Since I look like shit maybe I'll start back.'

126

'How long you been quit?'

'Not long after you left, I guess.'

She picked up a halfpiece of toast from his plate and took a bite.

'Can you tell me where you've been?'

'All over.'

'Before you hightailed it here.'

'Louisiana somewhere. Old sugar cane farm.'

'Whose house?'

'Some man.'

'Some man?'

'That's what I said.'

'You have a house right here.'

'Do I?'

'You're sure as hell sitting in it right now.'

Jace had moved off the couch and closer to the television. He stood right in front now with his finger touching the screen as a handsome man and a beautiful woman kissed in the smoky light of a sunset.

'What kind of shit are you in?' he asked.

'The kind that would make you start drinking again.'

'Is he dead?'

'Why would you ask me that?'

'Because you know the same things I know about where we live now. Not to mention you can't answer to where he is which means you don't know who he's with or what he's doing. And you're clearly running from something or you wouldn't have called me. Feels about like that Western on the television except for the happy ending.'

She picked up the coffee mug but didn't drink. Turned it in her hands.

'You don't need to worry,' she said. 'We won't stay long.'

'You can stay here as long as you want.'

It surprised them both when he said it and they exchanged a brief and awkward look. Then he couldn't take it anymore and he lit the cigarette. She reached across the table and took it from his mouth and said you can't smoke in the same room with a child and she dropped it in his water glass.

'There's a hurricane coming,' Wade said.

'There's always a hurricane coming.'

'I'm just saying, if you need somewhere to stay. This little house hasn't been knocked down yet.'

Jace had begun to mill around now. He pulled old hunting magazines from a basket next to the couch and made a pile on the floor.

'Do you remember Katrina?' she asked.

'Yeah. Why do you ask about that one?'

'It's the one I've always heard people talk about like it was the beginning.'

'I guess it was the beginning. Felt like the end at the time.'

'Was I born?'

'No. Me and your momma were either about to get married or just had. Hard to remember. Used to mark things in life by what hurricane hit when but that's gotten muddled.'

'What's happened to the corn?'

He shook his head. Stood from his chair and walked to the coffee pot and poured the last into his cup.

'Don't never dry out enough to keep a crop. Just sits there sagging now.'

'What happened to the Cotherns?'

'They left about a year ago. Maybe more. Said the hell with it.'

The grand house of the landowners stood in a crumbled mess on the other side of the acreage. A stretching antebellum.

Large oaks giving shade to the wide windows and big porch until the storms began to knock the trees into and onto the house. The family repaired the damage once, twice, three times. When the roof ripped off they packed up and left, telling Wade if the corn was ever a producing crop again they'd be back but they were heading where it was dry. Wherever that was. And by the way, there's no more payroll but you can stay where you are.

'I don't guess you go offshore no more,' she said.

'That's been over a pretty good while.'

He joined her again at the table. He pushed his plate toward her and asked if she wanted the last strip of bacon.

'I ain't hungry,' she said again.

'You look like you got some catching up to do.'

'I'm fine.'

Jace sat on the floor, ripping pages from a magazine.

'When is it supposed to be here?'

'What?'

'The storm.'

'Don't know. A week or so, I guess.'

'Why don't you leave?' she asked.

'Well. This is our home.'

'You still think of it that way?'

'How else should I think of it?'

'What do you do for work?'

'You'd probably call it stealing.'

'Is it?'

'Maybe. What do you do for work?'

'Raise that baby.'

'And what about him?'

'You can say his name. It ain't gonna kill you.'

'It might.'

'Say it and I'll answer.'

He shifted in his chair. Leaned back and folded his arms.

'What does Holt do for work?'

She shrugged.

'That's what I figured.'

'You don't know everything you think you know.'

'I know enough.'

Jace moved from magazine to magazine, tearing the pages into strips. Then he stood and turned redfaced and looked at his mother.

'I don't guess you got any diapers,' she said.

'No. But I know where to get some,' he said and he rose from the chair.

He grabbed his keys and wallet from the counter and asked her if they needed anything else. She only shook her head.

'All right,' he said. 'I'll get some groceries. I'm about out.'

'Okay.'

He crossed the room and opened the door. He wanted to turn and tell her don't run off. But he didn't. He only glanced over his shoulder at Jace and then Jessie and then he pulled out another cigarette and stuck it in his mouth as he walked down the steps and toward his truck where he was greeted with a big yellow sun. A sun that would not last.

28

WHEN HOLT ROSE FROM THE truck seat the morning had arrived. A solitary cow grazed across the field and a V of ducks passed above and he smacked himself on the cheeks and shook his head as he remembered all that had happened in the long night.

He got out of the truck and looked into the bed and found a pair of kneehigh rubber boots. He pulled them on and then he searched the cab for shotgun shells and he found a few scattered underneath the seat. The wind blew cold and the morningbirds awakened and sang little songs as the sun topped the horizon and he wondered if Jessie and Jace had made it out alive.

He didn't know how but he had been seen leaving the road in Delcambre that led to the house they had been hiding in deep in the cane field. And when the two vehicles skidded to a stop in the parking lot at the Dollar General and the men chased him around the building and tackled him and dragged him and tossed him into a trunk, he knew they were going to the house next. And Jessie and Jace would be slaughtered in the name of the keys.

He climbed in and cranked the truck and returned to the highway. He saw the marker for State Line Road and then in a few more miles he slowed as he approached the sign that read

LOUISIANA. He stopped. Tapped his fingers on the steering wheel. Turned around.

In ten minutes he came to the sign for Osyka and he knew where he was. He rolled through the only two stop signs in the dormant community. The handful of buildings seemed gray even in daybreak and blue tarps covered damaged rooftops of empty houses. A grimy school bus with a flat tire sat parked in front of an elementary school where kudzu climbed the brick and reached into the broken windows like the tentacles of reclamation.

A single speck of light interrupted the melancholy. Holt stopped the truck in the middle of the road and stared at the house. It was short and square. No vehicles. A pine tree fallen across the side yard. A bicycle and a tricycle under the carport. A light shining in the front room. He imagined going inside and finding warmth and food and a dial tone when he picked up the telephone. He imagined calling Wade's house and Jessie answering and saying we're okay. We're okay. He didn't believe she was there but it was the only phone call he knew to make.

But then he did not imagine them with Wade but he saw them lying lifeless, their bodies dumped across the nubs of sugar cane and his sense of selfishness erupted. Risking them for a set of keys that led to God knows what. Don't none of it matter if they're dead, he thought. Or if they're lost and running or if they were thrown into the back of a van like I was. The moment has come and gone when you could keep them safe and I hope you're happy. Christ almighty I hope you're happy.

I'm not happy and I'm never gonna be happy and I never been happy except with her and him and even if I find a magic child or a pot of gold with these goddamn keys I still probably won't be happy and I might not even have the keys no more if she didn't have time to grab them or if they got her before she even knew they were there.

He stepped out of the pickup carrying the shotgun and the old man's rubber boots squeaking as he walked along the driveway and to the door under the carport. He expected the door to be locked but when he turned the knob the door opened and he walked inside calling to anybody who might be home to settle down and don't do nothing stupid. I ain't here to hurt nobody but I will if I have to and yeah I got a gun and if you got one too then there ain't no use in us shooting each other. All I want is to use the phone if there is such a thing. I swear to God that's all I want. The carport door opened into a laundry room with no washer or dryer and he passed through a kitchen and then a living room. No furniture. Stained carpet. He moved down the short hallway. A couple of packed boxes left behind in one of the bedrooms. The house smelled musty and damp and he turned the light off in the living room. He stared at the telephone line that ran from the wall and lay across the carpet.

Without a thought he fired a shot into the ceiling, the drywall exploding and raining down in chalky fragments. His ears rang and his stomach turned in hunger and dejection and fear and withering bile and as the ringing calmed and he raised the shotgun to fire again for the pure and simple exaltation of being able to, he heard the bump in one of the bedrooms.

He looked toward the hallway. Waited. Another bump. He moved, the shotgun pointed. There was a bedroom door on each side and he stopped and called I swear I won't hurt you. He poked the barrel of the shotgun into the doorway on the right and then eased in. Nothing in the bedroom and nothing in the open closet.

He crossed into the other bedroom and he saw the sliding closet doors closed. And then he heard the bump again.

'Come out,' he said.

Another bump. The door rattled.

'I said come out and do it slow.'

He reached and put his hand on the sliding door.

'You better not fucking move.'

When he pulled back the door a raccoon as big as a dog jetted between his legs and his trigger finger jerked and the shotgun fired into the wall, the startled animal and the unexpected blast knocked him off balance and he backpedaled awkwardly until finally falling on his ass. He quickly sat up and gathered himself and aimed the shotgun at the closet as if expecting something bigger and badder and more hairy but he only saw the nest of straw and weeds of the blackeyed bandit. The dim light from the hole in the side of the house bathed the closet floor.

He shook his head. Mumbled to himself. Smoke bled from the shotgun barrel and dust and insulation floated from the hole in the wall. He rose to his feet and when he stood he saw the telephone on the top shelf of the closet. He took it down and held it. The phone was pink and decorated with stickers of flowers and rainbows and it had been either outgrown or forgotten.

He returned to the living room and leaned the shotgun against the wall. Then he picked up the telephone line and plugged it into the pink phone. He lifted the receiver.

A dial tone.

He had to think a second but he remembered the number to Jessie's house. Wade's house. He pushed the digits and heard the ringing. And it rang and rang and he was about to hang up when someone picked up on the other end. He waited for a hello but there was only silence. So he didn't speak. Then finally he heard Wade's voice.

'Don't you even fucking think about coming here.'

There was a click and Holt hung up. He lay back on the foul carpet and stared at the hole he had shot in the ceiling and the exhaustion and desperation and relief all washed over him and he began to cry, knowing they were alive and knowing they were safe.

But there was no time for that.

He pulled it together. There was nothing to do but go there and face Wade and try to explain what the hell was going on. Maybe if Wade believed they were in some kind of danger he would relent. Maybe.

He stood up and passed back through the hallway. At the end of the hallway were little marks on the wall that grew higher and higher, the growth of a child labeled with dates. Four years of getting taller. Four years of a mother or a father measuring her and drawing the new line and Holt touched the marks and heard the parents telling her how tall she was getting and what a big girl she was and he saw the little girl smiling and looking with pride at the new mark but now there were only echoes in this house and in so many other houses that had been abandoned. He leaned the shotgun against the wall and touched the scars on the back of his neck and for the first time in a long time he tried to remember the face of his own mother. He tried to form her eyes and nose and cheek but it would not come. She had drifted deep into his memory, growing vague and shapeless. He could not see her and he could not hear her but he could feel the heat on his back and he could hear his own screams and he could smell the smoke and gasoline and he could see the drunk scowl of the man she had made him call dad and with his eyes closed and his hands pressing his scars he imagined the little girl who owned the pink phone coming out of her room and down the hallway and taking his hand and telling him it's okay and when he opened his eyes again his hand had moved from his neck and he was touching the wall where she had stood and been measured and in that moment he wanted more than anything in the world to have a house where Jace could stand against the wall and he could mark his height year after year and tell him how proud he was of him and see the satisfaction in his small eyes. But all of it was worlds away.

He moved his hand from the wall. Go get them, he thought. Throw the keys in whatever river or pond or lake or puddle you can find and then run. Run north or east or west. Anywhere but south. Get them and go and it doesn't matter if the keys open heaven's gates just go get them and run and try to live some kind of life that is different from the one you have been living and it's a goddamn miracle you haven't gotten them killed. Go and get them and leave this place to evolve into whatever hell it is destined to become.

He lifted the shotgun. He passed through the house. Pausing and looking around and imagining what he and Jessie and Jace might look like in a real house with a real life, bits of laughter and the clanging of dishes being washed in the sink after a big meal and music coming from a radio on a bookshelf and a baseball glove and bat lying in the middle of the floor and cold beer in the refrigerator and sunlight through the windows and a comfortable couch to fall asleep on while a late night movie flashed on the television. It all seemed like some dream but he knew there were such people who did such things. And he was not one of them. He was holding a shotgun and he was hungry and hurt and trying to evade evil and he knew he had brought it all on himself and he had brought it all on Jessie and Jace and he was pretty goddamn sure he had brought it all on the old man who had saved him from the van and he now fired into the ceiling once again, as if it was possible to expel regret from the end of a shotgun barrel.

29

W HEN WADE RETURNED FROM TOWN Jessie and Jace were outside. Jace sat on his mother's shoulders and they stood three rows deep in the corn. The wind pushed the yellowbrown stalks and the boy reached for the wilted leaves as Jessie walked along a row, her shoes caked with mud. Wade rolled past them and the boy pointed at him from his mother's shoulders but Jessie kept her eyes down to the waving shadows of the windswept stalks.

He carried the bags inside and set them on the kitchen counter. He bought the only two packs of diapers and then he grabbed whatever else he could find from the shelves. Sometimes the market had food and sometimes it didn't and when it did he had learned to get as much as he could. He unpacked bologna and milk and orange juice and cookies and a carton of cigarettes. He had grabbed a box of Cheerios because he remembered Jessie eating them by the handfuls and he thought Jace might do the same. There was burger meat and pudding cups and rice and frozen vegetables and powdered donuts. It was more food than had been in the house in a long time and he felt some satisfaction in filling the refrigerator and cabinets no matter how odd the assortment.

He wadded the empty bags and stuck them in the garbage can and was heading for the door to join them in the sunshine when the phone rang. He looked back across the room. He had been surprised already by the voice of his daughter on the other end of the line and as he stared at the phone now and listened to it ring he could not help but think some hand of fate had dialed again. He pushed back the curtain and peeked outside and they had come out of the corn and Jessie was chasing Jace around the yard.

He let the curtain fall and he approached the telephone. It kept ringing and ringing and he wanted to do anything other than answer. But it wasn't going to stop. When he reached it he put his hand to the receiver and held it there. The ringing a small vibration against the flesh of his palm.

He picked it up. He didn't speak. The person on the other end of the line didn't speak. The silence of everything. Outside Jace squealed in laughter and Wade raised his eyes toward the window. He shifted his feet. His blood rising. An anger resurrected. And then he squeezed the receiver as if to choke the life away and he said don't you even fucking think about coming here and he slammed the receiver onto its cradle.

He stood there a moment. Waiting for the phone to ring again. Sucking in his breath. His muscles tightened with the anxiety, knowing Holt knew where they were and he was coming this way.

The phone remained silent. He let out the breath he was holding and walked across the room. He opened the door and walked down the steps and into the yard. He looked at Jessie and Jace as they shifted between the cornrows, a daughter and a grandson that did not exist when he closed his eyes last night. But here they were, playing underneath a high sun. He lifted his eyes to the sky. The blue above and reaching toward the east. The land brushed in gold. But the wind pushed and Wade turned and looked toward the west where a gathering of nickelgray clouds waited like patient predators.

30

OVERNIGHT THE WEATHER CHANGED. THE clear sky and crisp air had been pushed away, the temperature rising forty degrees and the air grown thick and stale. The morning covered in shades of gray like a shroud of remembrance.

Wade had only slept in intervals and he was awake at first light when he heard Jessie and Jace in the other room. Her muted voice and then tiny laughter. He climbed out of bed and stopped in the hallway, holding his ear to the door. The sounds just on the other side of a mother and child lost in one another.

He made coffee and then he walked outside and was mugged by the shift in the air. He knew what it meant. The humid calm that felt like some environmental purgatory, a holding before the judgment of the storm.

He walked around the side of the house to where the trailer sat. It was covered in HVAC units in all shapes and sizes. Big ones from big houses that took several men to move and smaller units the size of suitcases taken from windows. A full load strapped down and ready to be delivered and paid out. Money he didn't feel like he was in a rush for two days ago that now felt important.

When he came back around the house, Jessie was leaning in the open door of the hatchback.

'Where you going?' he asked.

'Nowhere,' she said. 'Just looking.'

'For what?'

She shrugged.

'That looks like a good enough little car. Needs a good cleaning.'

'It ain't going to get one,' she said and she closed the door.

'How long you had it?'

'It's not mine,' she said. 'I borrowed it.'

'From who?'

'I didn't ask.'

She walked up the steps and into the house and closed the door behind her. Wade shook his head. Rubbed his eyes. He wondered what it would be like to get into a fight with her on his side. How much damage they could do together if they put all their energy against a common foe. How quickly they could clear a barroom. She was as unflinching as a stone and he could not remember a time she had been any different and he was pretty sure she would say the same damn thing about him.

And that explained it to him. She is just like you. That is all you taught her and that is all she knows. Hide it. Whatever it is hide it and believe you are right no matter fucking what.

He went back inside and Jessie and Jace were sitting on the couch. Jace held a coffee mug with his small hands, a little milk mustache across his upper lip. He took another drink and handed it to Jessie and she asked if he was hungry. He didn't answer but slid down from the couch and walked to the television and pointed at it. Jessie picked up the remote from the couch arm and turned it on.

'I have to go to town and get us some stuff,' she said.

'What do you have to get?'

'Everything. We didn't exactly pack.'

'Eat first.'

'All right.'

Wade moved to the kitchen counter and poured two cups of coffee. He handed her a cup and pulled a chair from the table and slid it over next to the couch.

'What's that big box in the back of your closet?' she asked.

'What big box?'

'The only big box in there. Whose stuff is that? Hers?'

'What are you doing digging around in my closet?'

'I wasn't. Me and Jace were playing hide-and-seek yesterday when you went to town and he got in your closet and crawled over in the box and pulled the flap over his head.'

He nodded. Sipped the coffee.

'Well,' she said.

'It's just stuff.'

'It's a big box.'

'You said that.'

She shook her head at him. Crossed one leg over the other.

'Did you notice how it feels outside?' he said.

'Yeah. Nasty.'

'Probably won't be but a few days until it gets here.'

'I ain't worried about that right now. I'm worried about clean clothes and toothbrushes.'

'You still have some clothes in your bedroom.'

She raised her eyes in thought. She had left this house the same way she had arrived. Without regard for anything but the clothes on her back and what was in her pockets.

'Yeah. I guess I do.'

'You look about the same size.'

'I might be. I wasn't for a while.'

'How big did you get?'

'About usual, I guess. He didn't weigh much.'

'Were you in a hospital?'

'What?'

'A hospital. Did you have him in a hospital?'

'Where the hell else would I have him?'

'Shit I don't know. Nothing you could say right now would surprise me.'

She stood from the couch. Walked into the hallway and into her bedroom. Wade listened as the closet doors slid open and hangers shuffled and dresser drawers opened and slammed shut. She then reappeared and sat down again.

'I guess I can make do for now. But he don't have nothing.'

'You need some money?' Wade said. He stood and went into the kitchen and poured Cheerios into a bowl. He then set them down on the floor next to Jace, who was lying on his back and staring at the screen.

'Here,' he said to the boy. 'You got to eat. You know that?'

Jace sat up. Reached into the bowl and picked out a little circle and studied it.

'Go ahead. It's good,' Jessie said.

Jace stuck it in his mouth. Chewed. Thought. Chewed again. Then he reached into the bowl for more.

They watched him eat. Drinking their coffee. The phone rang in Wade's head. He imagined Holt out there somewhere, getting closer. And he felt the weight of the silence they had shared on the line. He wanted to make up some excuse to sit at the end of the road and wait for him and then send him back to wherever he came from but that had never worked before and it wasn't going to work now.

'What you want to eat?'

'Nothing,' she said. 'I changed my mind.'

'You need to eat something.'

'I will when I'm ready.'

Wade moved to the sink and poured out the coffee and set the cup on the counter.

'You can go to town but first I have to go back out,' he said.

'What for?'

'I need to go and gather some scrap at the old mall. They're gutting it.'

'Why now?'

'Because they take a break from the work whenever a hurricane is coming and if I don't go now somebody will beat me to it. That's how we eat around here.'

'You should have done it yesterday.'

'I was getting food. For my unexpected guests.'

'Fine. Just hurry back,' she said. And there was something in the sound of her voice. Something that made him think she meant it. That she didn't want them to be alone any longer than they had to be.

31

THE EDGEWOOD MALL WAS NEXT to the interstate and once upon a time it had been a springboard for economic growth. Chain stores and restaurants sprang up around it and there was the addition of new traffic lights and the streets stayed paved and property values went up in the neighborhoods surrounding the commerce. In the summer groups of awkward teenagers hung around the food court and stared at other groups of awkward teenagers. Fashion shows were held in the concourse. Santa Claus had a long line during the holidays.

The sign that stood among the shrubs and spotlights of the entrance no longer read EDGEWOOD MALL. Now the hand-carved letters of the weatherbeaten sign were covered with a banner that flapped in the wind and read COMING SOON: SOUTH MISSISSIPPI REGIONAL STORM FACILITY.

Wade circled the parking lot and he was right. The work had stopped with the forecast and there was plenty of good stuff filling the dumpsters as the transformation from commercial mall to hurricane hub was slow but steady. He could never figure out why there seemed to be no urgency but it meant that the construction site would give to him for many more months. Maybe years. He pulled the pickup alongside a long roll-off dumpster. He grabbed his gloves from the seat and he stepped out of the truck and climbed up onto the hood to where he could see in.

In between the mildewed insulation and drywall and chunks of concrete he eyed what he wanted. Copper pipes and air duct pipes. Some folding chairs. Big mobs of old wiring. He gave a quick scan around the parking lot, not wanting to have to deal with security guards who took themselves seriously and had run him off before like he was some scavenging and smelly dog.

Just hurry back, he heard Jessie say.

Wade looked around the changed scene. Out of a dozen restaurants, just two remained open. The traffic lights only blinked in a cautious yellow now, never enough circulation for the exchange of stop and go. A gas station sign read NO GAS HERE BEER AND LIQUOR ONLY.

He pulled on his gloves and he hopped down into the dumpster and went to work.

32

WADE RETURNED WITH THE CLAMOR of a modernday tinker. Jessie was looking in the refrigerator when she heard the rattles and clanks and she watched from the kitchen window as Wade parked the truck next to the cattle trailer. He stood in the truck bed and lifted out the scraps and tossed them onto what she believed was already an impressive accumulation of junk. His head and shirt were both drenched with sweat and she thought he seemed like a younger man as he worked. As if he had the ability to be something different when he was in motion.

After the truck bed was emptied he climbed out and took off his gloves. He opened the door and tossed them into the cab and then he lit a cigarette. He wiped his wet face with his wet shirt and he stared at the trailer as if calculating and he seemed satisfied by the haul. Jessie jerked back from the window when his eyes rose and he headed for the door.

When he came into the kitchen she was standing there with her hand out.

'The keys are in it,' he said.

'Okay. Jace is asleep back there on your bed.'

'All right.'

He stepped to the sink and filled a glass of water and chugged. She stepped past him and was almost to the door when he told her to wait. He opened a drawer and he reached in and pulled out a fold of cash. He counted off eighty dollars and he stepped to her and held it out. She took it and then she stared at him.

'What?' he said.

'When I get back I want to talk to you. Really talk to you. I'll tell you what's been going on. But you got to get ready for it. And that's what I want you to do when I'm gone. Get ready for it.'

He nodded.

'I'm serious, Wade.'

'I'll get ready then.'

'Because the second you start preaching or telling me what the hell I should have done or what I should do, I'll be done talking.'

He nodded again. Then she walked out. He moved to the window and watched her climb in the truck and drive away.

Get ready, he thought. I'd like to know how in the hell she expects me to do that. He drank another glass of water and then he peeled off his shirt and tossed it toward the washing machine. And then he moved to the telephone and unplugged the cord from the receiver.

33

JESSIE DROVE THE WINDING HIGHWAY with her arm propped on the windowsill. She sang along with the radio and it was as if she had been transported back in time. Only a few years earlier she had been a teenager who rode these roads with other teenagers, laughing and gossiping and making up dumb lyrics to songs and there were no boys or men or surprise children to screw it all up. Not yet.

The air was warm through the window and she wrestled out of her coat and tossed it across the bench seat. Turned the volume up. Turned off the highway onto a bumpy county road where the barbed wire ran along with the bends and tree limbs hung low and flicked the antenna of the truck. She drove casually, the weight she carried flaking away and falling across the hills and slipping down the creek banks. No one passed her on the backroads. No one seemed to be living in the houses. No one seemed to be driving the tractors that sat parked with the grass grown high around their big tires. She came to the top of the hill and slowed, expecting a mobile home to be sitting off to the right, a pond next to it. A pond where she and the girl who lived there would meet boys in the middle of the night and drink from quarts of beer and look at the stars and make the boys believe they had a chance. She slowed and then stopped and looked along the driveway. I can't even remember her damn name, she thought. But even if she could she was not going to pull into the driveway and not going to say hello because a swingset was next to the mobile home and two tricycles were lying on their sides by the front door.

She drove on. There was a serenity on these backroads that she had not felt in a long time. A farreaching stretch of emotion had wound up inside her, a great ball of unrest that had spun fast in a short amount of time. The way she had been drawn to Holt and with it came the notion of escaping this place. The anxiety between Wade and Holt and Wade suddenly wanting to be a protective father. The unexpected heartbreak of leaving home though she hated it. The confusion when Holt told her about being chased. About the keys. About the Temple of Pain and Glory. The surprise and doubt when she found out she was pregnant. The unknown of town to town, place to place, the uncertainty of strange faces, always wondering if they were looking for Holt. Always wondering if it was time to run. The intensity of labor and childbirth and the newborn in her arms and the depths of love and fear that came with it. Being hungry. Praying to God the baby wasn't hungry. Wondering when the next hurricane would come and wondering if it would be the one that none of them could survive as if a Bible story may come to life and refresh the earth with one great and mighty storm.

She felt none of that now. She rode across bridges that were one car wide and she tapped her fingers on the steering wheel to the rhythm of the radio and when she looked at herself in the rearview mirror they were not the eyes of the woman but the eyes of the girl and she liked the way those eyes looked back, as if the whole world remained available to her. She felt the warmth of the wind and she was surrounded by gray but she ignored the dull tones as she instead remembered the blue skies of summer. The pink of a sunset. The brush of lavender on the edge of dusk.

And then she remembered the times she and Wade had laid in the bathtub with a mattress pulled over them. The deafening winds and driving rains of a storm. The schools closing for weeks. The flooding. No electricity and boiling water and the friends who left with their families and found new homes in safer places and she stomped on the gas when the bad cut off the good and she leaned around the curves and lost her stomach over a hill and when she swerved to dodge an armadillo and her tires rode the ridge of a ditch before she yanked it back and managed to keep the truck on the road, she decided that was enough.

She stopped the truck in the middle of the road. You will ride and be the girl or you will not ride, she thought. She got out of the truck and walked around in the road. She caught her breath and lit a cigarette and fought the bad thoughts but one remained.

Where was Holt?

Nothing about her life seemed real now as she stood alone in the countryside in the one part of the world she knew. As if her memories belonged to a story she had been told.

She climbed back into the truck and drove on, moving in the direction of town. There was one thing that was real and that was the little boy and he needed clothes and it hit her right between the eyes how bad Jace needed a place to keep those clothes and a bed to sleep in and a room to call his own and she felt herself sink as she thought of the wild chase she had taken him on in his short life and how she had to grab him and run through the woods while men fired shotguns because they wanted his father and they would always want his father as long as he held on to the keys and what the hell were you thinking.

She banged the steering wheel. Screamed out of the window. She came to a four-way stop and she dropped her head back against the seat and let out a great sigh.

She then turned the truck around in the road and went back the other way, trying to remember how to get there and missing a turnoff and doubling back and then making the turn onto a thinner, bumpier cutthrough that took her on a steady rise and through a turn where broken limbs lay across the fence row and fallen trees rotted in pastures and she moved up and up until she reached the top of the hill. She slowed, then pulled off the road and parked the truck at the wroughtiron gate.

Jessie stared across the gate at the small gathering of headstones in the quaint hilltop cemetery. She then opened the door and got out. Vines twisted through the iron bars and she tugged and tore them away as she pulled open the gate. The ground was thick with leaves and limbs. The headstones were no longer slick but weathered with time and inattention, black streaks and grime and bird shit. A dozen graves lay in two neat rows and Jessie walked past them and to the solitary headstone that rested apart at the edge of the cemetery. It was flanked by red maples and remained in shadow in all but the winter months when streaks of light slashed between leafless limbs.

She sat down with her mother. She leaned her back against the headstone and closed her eyes and listened. Birds called and sang and squirrels rustled through the leaves and she felt herself getting sleepy. No need to rush or run or fear. Behind her eyes there was a world where she had helped her mother in the kitchen and sat with her on the porch and read a book and listened to her sing happy birthday and sat very still while her mother braided her hair. There was a world where she and Holt and Jace lived in a normal house with normal furniture and had normal meals at normal times. There was a world where there were great reaches of sky that only gave the sun and the stars and the moon. And there was a world where she and her mother and father could be together. At least for a little while.

34

THE PARKING LOT WAS MOSTLY empty. And so was the strip mall. Jessie remembered a grocery store and a Chinese restaurant and a department store that were no longer there. Their replacements were a tobacco store and Goodwill and vacant spaces. On one side of the parking lot a man sat on the tailgate of his truck with his hat pulled down low on his head, holding a sign that read MAN AND TRUCK FOR HIRE.

She walked into Goodwill and took a shopping cart and she moved through the wide aisles. The shelves had no particular order or pattern. Candlesticks next to coloring books. A volleyball next to a mismatched set of dishes. There was little order and fewer price tags. At the end of the aisles were tables where clothes were strewn about as if they had landed there in some game where employees tossed for distance.

She managed to find a pile of children's clothes. She scrounged through and dug out toddler pants and shirts of different sizes but that seemed to be in the ballpark of what Jace could wear. She found a denim coat she thought he would look cool in. A pair of little man workboots he would grow into. She moved through each table and uncovered what she could and then at the end of the tables was a row of bookshelves. The shelves were littered with books and records and toys. She found four Dr. Seuss books, some building blocks, and a gladiator doll and she felt herself smiling when she set them all into the buggy with the clothes. She moved to the front of the store where a young woman sat on a stool behind a counter, watching a small television.

Jessie began to shift items from the cart to the counter. The woman turned down the volume on the television and rose from the stool.

'Jessie?' she said.

Jessie lifted her eyes.

'Charlotte?'

'Holy shit,' the young woman said. She moved around the counter and hugged Jessie and then they stood back from one another. Sizing each other up. As if making sure they were who they thought they were.

'I didn't think you were around here no more,' Charlotte said. She wore a baggy flannel shirt and too much eye shadow and her big pile of hair spilled from a loose ponytail.

'I'm not.'

'It don't look like it to me.'

'I guess you could say I'm passing through.'

Charlotte returned behind the counter and slapped her hands together and pointed at the toddler clothes.

'Looks like you been up to something since I saw you last.'

'Yeah, a little something.'

'But Lord. You're still as skinny as ever. If not more than you used to be.'

'I can't tell if you're being nice or mean.'

'Who's the daddy? One of our local heroes?'

'Not even close.'

'Good for you. They have a tendency to lose their steam, I'm finding out.'

'I don't guess you're talking about Bobby are you?'

'Course.'

'How is he?'

'Fine. Aggravated. He can't get no work. It wears on him and me both.'

'Are y'all married?'

She holds out her hand and shows a silver ring with a tiny emerald stone.

'Going on a year. Don't be fooled by the ring, I got to keep telling people.'

'Didn't he give you that in high school?'

'He did. And I told him when we can buy wedding rings we will but there wasn't no sense in worrying about it now.'

'That's a lucky boy, Charlotte. He know that?'

'Sometimes.'

They kept chatting as Jessie emptied the cart and Charlotte sorted through the items.

'I didn't see prices on all of it,' Jessie said.

'I know it. Some of it has stickers. Some of it has prices written on tags. Some of it has nothing and we mostly make it up as we go. Unless it figures that if it doesn't have a price it must not cost nothing,' she said and she winked at Jessie. She then dropped the unmarked clothes into a bag without charging.

'Too bad you don't work at the bank. You could really hook me up.'

'Sometimes I think about robbing one. Don't seem like it would be that hard. Does it? Not a big bank but one of those little trailer banks that sit on the edge of town.'

'I ain't surprised that's what you'd think.'

'Really, Jessie.'

'Really.'

Charlotte finished with the clothes and then she added up the books and toys. She stuffed it all into one large bag and handed it over the counter and Jessie paid her.

'I'm hardly ever surprised by anybody showing up anymore,' Charlotte said. 'It's always about people leaving.'

On the television screen behind the counter an American flag waved and a redfaced man in the corner of the screen pumped his fist and delivered his news with great vehemence.

'Why do you watch that shit?' Jessie said and nodded at the television.

Charlotte glanced over her shoulder at the screen and then scanned the store. She leaned toward Jessie and lowered her voice.

'Boss makes us leave it on. I think he's trying to brainwash us.'

'It'll likely happen if you keep staring at it.'

'You heard what they been saying about down here lately?'

'Down where?'

'Here. Mississippi and Louisiana and bunch of other places close to the coast.'

'What?'

'Been saying if the storms don't quit then this part of the country might just get shut down.'

'Shut down?'

'That's what they say. Said it costs too much to keep it going but as far as I can see I damn sure don't recognize no money being spent. I don't figure it'll happen but a lot of shit that I don't figure on happens anyway.'

'That man right there don't look like he knows anything about down here.'

Charlotte peeked at the screen again.

'It's some others that come on there. Between talking about God and guns they manage to mention the weather every now and then. I tell you what, I don't know how much longer me and Bobby can stay here. It's home and all but it's tough. He can't get on a crew nowhere, nobody's building nothing. And when nobody's building nothing there's no plumbing or concrete work or framing and that's about all he knows how to do.'

She paused. Her eyes moved from Jessie and toward the storefront windows. Her bottom lip trembled so slightly.

'He even said he might start selling cars but can you imagine that? Him standing in the sales lot waiting all day for somebody to walk up and pretend they want to buy a car. I just don't know what there is to gain anymore by being here. It's only a shell.'

Jessie reached across the counter and took her hand. Charlotte's eyes came back to her.

'Me and you should ride around and drink a beer,' Jessie said.

Charlotte nodded. Squeezed Jessie's hand.

'You're lucky, Jessie.'

'How so?'

'You got away from here.'

Jessie smiled at her. She wanted to give her friend the reality of things but it didn't seem like that would help either of them.

'So will you,' she said.

Jessie picked up the bag and Charlotte walked with her to the door and held it open for her.

'If you stay around, come back and see me. We can ride around and drink that beer,' Charlotte said.

Jessie nodded and then she turned from her and crossed the parking lot to the truck. A great melancholy fell over her as she walked. She wanted to look back at Charlotte and she didn't want to. Because she knew that Charlotte would be watching her from behind the window, somehow admiring her and there was nothing to admire. She set the bags inside the cab and she took the cigarette pack from the seat and tapped one out. She held it between her lips and flicked the lighter but as the tip turned red she pulled it from her mouth and tossed it away. No more time for that, she thought. No more time for nothing.

35

HOLT HAD PARKED OFF THE highway and into a patch of grass. He then walked through the woods and came around on the backside of the cornrows. In the distance he could see the peak of the roofline of Wade's house above the dead stalks.

He moved between the stalks. He was exhausted and hurt and he moved slowly out of both necessity and care and his doubts shifted with each step. She's not there. How could she be? But hadn't Wade's tone given it away? His threat meant she was there. No way is she there.

When he got close enough that he could see between the stalks he stopped and took notice. A hatchback he did not recognize. No sign of the truck he remembered Wade driving. A trailer piled with used HVAC units. He slipped through, a little closer. Moving to where he could get his eyes on the porch and front door.

He waited. Nothing.

He knelt down. So tired. He tried to remember the last time he had really slept or really eaten and it wasn't possible to figure it out. All he could think of was the darkness. The darkness of the blindfold they had put on him when they pounced and shoved him in the back of the car. The darkness of the waiting in the small closet where he could not stretch out his legs. The darkness of the back of the van and the darkness of night and the darkness of the voices of the men who handled him and drove the van and the darkness of the fragments they spoke in.

He lay down on his back in the cornrows. Fatigue crept over him as he watched the brown stalks sway against the flatgray sky and he stretched out his arms and legs and lay there motionless like a scarecrow pushed from its perch. His eyes closed and he felt his mind slip into sleep when the sound of the lawnmower engine rumbled across the silent land.

He sat up. Crawled further through the corn.

The sound came from the shed behind Wade's house and then the double doors of the shed opened. The nose of the riding mower appeared and Wade sat behind the wheel and Jace sat in his lap. Wade held the steering wheel with one hand and had his other wrapped around Jace and the mower wheeled out of the shed. A shriek of happiness came from Jace as Wade accelerated across the yard.

Holt fell flat to the ground when they turned in his direction. He watched as the lawnmower made loops and circled the house and then it headed for the road that split the crop. Holt scurried on his hands and knees deeper back into the stalks as the lawnmower approached and it passed by him without notice. The face of his son wild with excitement as he bounced in Wade's lap.

He looked toward the house and hoped for Jessie to come out of the door. Hoped for her to appear in the yard. But all was still. The sound of the lawnmower grew faint as Wade drove the crop road away from the house and Holt got to his feet. He stepped through the stalks and stood on the dirt road and watched them shrink in the distance.

He hurried toward the house. Limping and hurting but going as quickly as he could. Looking back over his shoulder.

He came to the hatchback and he opened the door and the bad smell hit him and reminded him of the rank and dour smell of the back of the van. The scent of captivity. He looked for anything that might say Jessie but the car was strange. He closed the door and checked down the road and then hurried to the house. He tripped up the last step and landed on his elbows but he sucked in the pain and rose again and when he flung open the door he did not step inside but instead called out.

'Jessie!'

Silence.

'Jessie! Are you in here?'

No reply.

He heard the hum of the lawnmower and knew it had turned around and was coming back toward the house. He stepped inside and closed the door behind him. He kept calling her name as he moved through the house as if she was only winning some game of cat-and-mouse and not somewhere else. He rushed into the hallway and looked into the bathroom and each bedroom and the hum of the lawnmower came closer and just as he was turning to head for the backdoor, he saw the bulky keys lying on the bed of Wade's room.

He stared at them. Listened to the lawnmower.

Then he left the room and left the keys. He crossed the front room and peeked between the curtains and Wade and Jace sped around the yard and Holt began to sink as he saw the child's happiness. A happiness he did not recognize. He moved from the curtain and limped across the room and past the kitchen and into the laundry room where a door opened to the back of the house. He eased out, listening for the direction of the lawnmower. When he felt it was safe he looked around the side of the house and the lawnmower moved away from him and he hurried across the yard and back into the cover of the cornstalks. He hid there and watched them. Trying to reason between staying or leaving. Wanting to see her and wanting to hold Jace but something about the peacefulness of what he observed was telling him to turn and pass through the corn and cross the woods and get in the truck and start driving and leave them right where they are.

He dropped his head. Pushed aside the stalks and began to move away, like some dejected spirit grown weary of the haunt. Jace shrieked again as Wade cut the wheel, the quick pulse of joy. Holt wanted to turn and look but he let it be and instead he remembered the day that Jessie had told Wade to go to hell and then she climbed in with Holt and the hurt of dejection that burned in Wade's eyes as he watched them go. Not one damn thing he could do about it other than watch and simmer. Now Holt knew this feeling.

He made it through the corn. Through the woods. He opened the door to the old man's truck and sat there without an answer. He then cranked the truck and backed out into the highway. He shifted into drive and eased along as if drifting toward the end of the earth. The stalks stood in their rows and the clouds sat in their sky and the birds sang in their trees and he envied them all. He drove mindlessly, his eyes affixed to the road ahead but his mind wandering into a deep cavern where there was only the dark and jagged space of solitude. In his daze he drifted from his lane and into the other and was snapped awake when a horn blared and he yanked the wheel to keep from colliding with the passing vehicle. It happened fast and the oncoming truck passed in a flash but his eyes caught the middle finger raised at him and caught the cussing face.

He slammed on the brakes and skidded to a stop in the middle of the road. Looked in the rearview mirror as Wade's truck sped away. Then he made fists and knocked them against his forehead. Opened his hands and slapped them against his cheeks. He then sat there, huffing and thinking. After a moment, he shifted into drive and drove on to the next crossing. At the crossing he turned the truck around and headed back toward the house.

36

JESSIE DROPPED THE GOODWILL CLOTHES into the washing machine and then she poured the last of the coffee. She walked out and sat down on the porch and the hum of the riding lawnmower rose and fell as Wade made laps around the house. Once Wade stopped in the yard and Jace slapped his hands and screamed for more and Wade shifted and they rode again.

Finally Wade drove back into the shed and killed the engine. It whirred and died out and then he carried Jace across the yard and up the steps and set him down by his mother.

'Was that fun?' she asked him.

'Wade,' he answered and he pointed.

'Yeah. Wade. He's a good driver.'

'Again.'

'We'll do it again in a little while,' Wade said. 'I might need to go get some gas.'

Jace crawled up in Jessie's lap.

'You have any luck in town?' Wade asked.

'I did okay.'

Wade walked back down the steps and into the yard and he sat on the hood of the hatchback. He lit a cigarette and wiped at his forehead.

'I'm ready whenever you are,' he said.

'For what?'

'To explain all the stuff you said you were going to explain when you got back.'

She looked away from him. Jace flopped down from her lap and slipped through the open door and went inside.

'He must be hungry,' she said.

Wade only smoked. Didn't push her. He knew what a ride to town could do. Particularly a long ride, which she had taken. He knew how your mind worked on the backroads.

'Can I ask you something first?' she said.

He nodded.

'How come you're still here?'

'What do you mean by here?'

'Down here.'

'Mississippi?'

'You don't have a job. None are coming. You steal people's air conditioners to stay fed.'

He drew on the cigarette. An irritation crossed his face but he had asked himself the same questions during the empty nights and it fell away.

'The weather,' he said.

'What?'

'Don't forget the weather. That's the cause of all this.'

'I didn't figure I had to say that part.'

'There's not much you can do about the weather.'

'I didn't ask you to change the weather. I asked why you stayed here with nothing to do and nobody to do it with.'

He stood from the hatchback and paced.

'Well?' she said.

He shrugged. Shook his head.

'I don't know other than I never been nowhere else.'

'So what?'

None of it made sense to her now. She had run off with Holt in a rage of youth and been enthralled with the movement and the desperation and the notion that she was a character in some wild ride of an adventure love story that would be told for ages to come. She looked at her hands and her fingers were long and bony and it hit her that she was still in the midst of her youth and she believed if she didn't get up and do something then it would be wasted in the squalor of the stormworld. She would wake up one day and be alone and thieving to survive like her father.

'You wouldn't be abandoning her,' she said.

'I didn't say I would be.'

'What are you afraid of?'

'I didn't say I was afraid of a damn thing.'

She stood. Crossed her arms and leaned against the porch rail. The air around them so still. The color so gray. A holding cell of life with the walls closing in.

'You know, all I ever wanted you to do was talk about her some. Tell me about her some. It wouldn't have mattered what you said. Any goddamn thing would have been good. Did you know that?'

Wade would not look at her. Could not give her any answers. He only paced and smoked with nothing to win.

'You got to know her. You got to be in the same room with her. Talk to her. That's more than I ever got. You ever think about that when you were stepping around me? Going offshore and leaving me here with whoever? Huh? You ever think you weren't the only one with a big hole shot right through your middle?'

'I don't want to talk about it,' he said.

'No shit, Wade. That's always been your problem.'

'What do you want me to say?'

She shook her head at him and felt the spin of time. He walked a circle and pretended he didn't know what the hell she was talking about and they were right back in the same spot they had always been.

'You decide what to say. I can't put words in your mouth or I would've started a long time ago.'

She turned and called into the open door for Jace. Then she sat down on the porch steps and dropped her head between her knees. Wade watched her. He thought of all the times he had seen her with her head hanging and her eyes wandering and all the times he did not say anything or cross the room to her and instead remained in the corridors of his own sorrow while his daughter sat alone.

'I'm sorry, Jessie.'

She didn't move.

'I'm sorry,' he said again. 'I'm sure it don't mean shit. But I am.'

She raised her head. Wade kept his eyes on his daughter, wanting her to believe it. She wore a vacant expression as if she did not know where she was or who she was with.

'I'm leaving,' she said. 'And by leaving I don't mean this house. I mean this town.'

'Going where?'

'Somewhere there's an ordinary life to be found. Somewhere I can send Jace to school. Somewhere I don't have to hear evacuation sirens.'

'That's a long list.'

'Quit acting like it don't exist. It used to be that way here.'

'I know,' he said. 'I know.'

Jace came back out of the door holding the box of Cheerios. 'How'd you get those?' she asked him.

'I left the box on the couch so he could grab it,' Wade said. The boy sat down on the porch and reached his arm down into the box and pulled out a handful. He then picked one and stuck it in his mouth.

'Go with us,' Jessie said.

When the words came out it surprised them both. Part of her thought to grab them back but she let them hang in the air. She wouldn't look at Wade but instead kept her eyes on Jace and waited to see if Wade would answer.

He stood dumbstruck. He glanced around as if maybe she had said it to someone else. That he heard it by mistake. But then the thoughts formed and they were as surprising as her offer. Yes, he thought. I will go. We will go.

'Are you being serious?' he said.

She nodded. Her eyes still on the boy. He walked over and sat down on the top porch step. Leaned his back against the post.

'I don't know that I could be more surprised by all this,' he said. 'But if you want to go I'll go with you. God knows I've sat here long enough.'

Then she turned to him. She shared his sharp eyes and sharp nose and she realized he might have been handsome. Maybe he still was beneath the stubble and hair he clearly cut himself. She had despised him for so long but in this moment of apparent truce he seemed to be an actual person. There were things that would always hurt. Things that could never heal. She only wanted to live from right now.

Neither of them recognized the vehicle approaching along the crop row. It moved slowly, as if being pushed by roadside Samaritans. When it came to the end of the corn, the truck stopped. The driver taking note of the scene.

Wade stood up. Walked down the steps and into the yard.

The truck then eased forward and as it came closer, Jessie

picked up Jace and joined Wade and they stood together as the truck came forward and shifted into park. Holt stared at them from behind the wheel.

'Don't ever say you couldn't be more surprised.'

'Yeah,' Wade said. Then he spit and lit another cigarette. 'I'll never say it again if I live to be a thousand.'

The truck door opened and Holt stepped out. The bruised face. The bloodstains on his ragged jeans. The ashen eyes. He held the door as if to keep from falling over but he did not have to worry about collapse as Jessie handed Jace off to Wade and she ran to Holt and wrapped her arms around him.

37

WADE HELD JACE AND WATCHED Jessie and Holt hold on to each other. She gingerly touched his cheeks and forehead. He dropped his head on her shoulder. They spoke in whispers and exchanged expressions of astonishment and relief. Jace wiggled in Wade's arms and he set the boy down and he began hustling toward them. Little arms reaching and little legs shifting. Holt saw him coming and he stepped around Jessie and met Jace as he stumbled and staggered on the uneven ground, sweeping the boy up in a cry of exhilaration just before he fell.

Wade stood there alone. When the reunion turned toward him, he walked to his truck and he got in and cranked it. They were climbing the porch steps and going inside as he drove away.

38

HOLT LAY ON HIS STOMACH, his back moving up and down in slow and rhythmic draws of breath. Jace lay next to him in the identical position. Jessie leaned in the doorway with her arms crossed and stared at them. The shadowed figure of watchfulness.

He had taken a shower and she had given him a pair of jeans and a shirt from Wade's closet and thrown his awful clothes into a barrel behind the house where Wade burned trash. She had fixed him something to eat and then he asked if Wade was going to let them stay there. She nodded. Where do you think he went? She shook her head. The evening became night and she kept opening the door and looking toward the road for Wade to return but there was only the dark. The sky draped in thick clouds that blotted out the moonlight and the rustle of the stalks blowing in the nightwind.

When Jace had fallen asleep they sat down on the couch together and he told her about it all. About being seen and snatched and days in a dark room and then being put into the van and the big swerve and the wreck and getting his hands on the shotgun and the old man helping him from the road and all of it.

'Where was it?' she asked.

'Not far from here.'

'What do you think that means?'

'It could mean something. It could mean nothing.'

'What did they say to you?'

'Nothing. Not a damn word. Nobody said a damn word to me about anything.'

'Nobody asked you about the keys?'

'No.'

'Was it Elser?'

'I don't know.'

'How the hell can you not know?'

'I'm telling you. Nobody talked to me. Nobody said nothing about nothing. I don't know what was going on. I don't understand any of it.'

Jessie had stood and paced around the room as he kept trying to explain, rubbing her hand up and down her thin arm and releasing sighs and hearing his voice but finding it hard to hear anything but the echo of the gunshots as she ran into the woods holding their son. When Holt finally went quiet she returned to him on the couch. They both sat slumped. Both eyed their own wobbly reflections in the blank screen of the television. Neither mustered a word for a long time and in the paltry lamplight the night seemed to sink into a timeless abyss. And then he said it.

'I know where the keys belong.'

She shifted her eyes from the television to Holt.

'What?'

'It's called the Bottom.'

'Why didn't you start with that?'

'Because it's hard to say out loud.'

'How come?'

'It just is. It's like admitting you know where to find the boogey man or the Easter Bunny.'

'I thought you said nobody talked to you.'

'I heard voices in whatever house I was in and then the men in the van talked about it. That's where we were going. Some place called the Bottom.'

'To do what?'

'I heard one say he'll talk when we get to the Bottom. He'll shit those keys right out.'

'What does that mean?'

'I didn't want to find out. I think they take a lot of people there.'

'These are not answers.'

'I don't know, Jessie. Whatever they were going to do with me seemed like a routine. The van was full of old clothes and shoes. It smelled like a goddamn grave.'

Jace let out a cry in his sleep. Jessie stood and moved toward the hallway but the child did not make another sound.

'It can't be far from here,' he said.

She did not return to the couch but walked into the kitchen and to the cabinet where Wade had always kept his liquor. She opened the cabinet and the bottle sat there but it was full and the seal unbroken. A strange testament to sobriety that she did not comprehend but there was much she did not comprehend. She took it down from the cabinet and unscrewed the cap and she poured into a glass. She returned to Holt and she sat down on the edge of the fireplace and stared into the shifting amber of the glass until he finally said I could use one of those too. She then drank and squeezed her eyes shut and let it burn down and then she handed him the glass and he finished it.

'I don't know what I thought was going to happen,' she said. She had shifted her knees to the side and she stared into the ash and soot of the hearth. 'One day I was sneaking cigarettes in the high school bathroom. The next day I was run off with you. And then you told me these wild stories about keys and revival meetings and the child of God and it seemed like the world had gone crazy. Just all out, batshit crazy. And I loved it. I wanted to be part of the craziness. I wanted to be part of the storm. I liked how it felt. I liked being a little bit afraid. But I don't like it no more. There's a little boy asleep in there and I won't let him grow up without his momma.'

'Why would he grow up without his momma?'

'Because this shit is going to get us killed. You ever think of that?'

'Yeah. This ain't new.'

'You're right. It's old. And it has got old quick.'

She reached and stuck her finger down into a mound of ash. She pushed it around, admiring the weightlessness. Holt stood from the couch and returned to the bottle and poured again. He drank half and then he came to her at the fireplace and handed her the glass. He stood in front of her and looked toward the window and the black between the blinds.

'I don't believe in a child of God,' he said.

She looked up at him. With his head turned toward the window she could see the scars on the back of his neck and she wondered if he would ever tell her how they got there. She wondered if there was such a thing as really knowing him. She turned up the glass and drank.

'Nobody does,' she said.

'Yes,' he said. 'Some do. I watched them. I heard them. Some of them cry over the very thought of the notion of some little girl hidden somewhere who has the miracle of Momma Nature. As crazy as it all sounds don't you wonder if there is something to believe? Something even beyond words. Does it have to be understood to be part of this world?'

'There is plenty I can see in every direction that I don't understand.'

'You know what I mean.'

'And you know what I mean,' she said. 'I don't care about what a bunch of headnodders worship. You could starve them to death and they'd thank you for the steak dinner. It is my own mystery why I am only now coming to this realization. It should be your mystery just as well.'

She drank again. Holt walked over to the window. He separated the blinds and looked out into the night.

'I don't know what to do,' he said.

'You know what to do. What you don't know is what you want to do.'

She had stood from the fireplace and walked a lap around the couch, swirling the bourbon in the glass. Holt removed his fingers from the blinds and they flicked back into place. He walked over to her and she kissed him and then he vanished in the shadows of the hallway. She had heard the bedroom door open and heard the creak of Wade's old headboard when Holt lay down next to Jace.

Now she watched them sleeping. Her head light from the bourbon. Her mind set on another life. She imagined a gathering of spirits just on the other side of the dark, beckoning to her with the knowledge of things to come. Among them was her mother.

She returned to the couch and sat down. She turned on the television, the electric light stretching across the room in a glowing rectangle. She watched without sound as a man wearing an apron stuck carrots and cucumbers and apples into a blender and then added a scoop of his magic powder and pushed a button. It blended down and he poured it into a glass and handed it to a young woman with the right curves and the right hair and makeup and she drank it and then turned to the audience with a lunatic grin and they responded with applause. The man kept blending different concoctions of fruits and vegetables and kept dumping on the magic powder to the delight of all who witnessed. Jessie sipped the bourbon away, simultaneously repulsed by and envious of the performance on the screen. She set the empty glass on the arm of the couch and stood up and walked to the door and opened it again and stared out. One last look for Wade.

She closed the door. She took two steps away then she turned back and locked it. She was reaching to turn off the television when the scroll began across the bottom of the screen.

MANDATORY EVACUATION ORDER IS
NOW IN EFFECT FOR THE FOLLOWING
COUNTIES...

She stepped back. Watched the county names pass. The familiar locations across lower Mississippi and the Gulf Coast. She waited to see Pike and then it slid by in its usual alphabetical slot.

She changed the channel. More mindless middle of the night programming. Another scroll demanding evacuation. The shifting light of the screen flashed on her face as she stared at the scroll and the last words she noticed were POSSIBILITY OF TORNADOES as she turned off the television and sat there in the dark.

39

WADE WAS CROSSEYED DRUNK BY nightfall. It hadn't been what he was after when he turned off the crop road and onto the highway, driving with his elbow propped on the door and his hand against his forehead in some pathetic contemplation of life. Just as you begin to ease across the bridge the goddamn thing will start to burn right underneath your feet, he thought. She left pissed off because you made her pissed off and now she's standing in your house with her child and with that son of a bitch and you were about a minute away from getting her back. About a fucking minute.

He burned bitter then, the image of the three of them embracing foremost in his mind. Smiling together. An actual family. Something he didn't see coming. He never saw anything coming and his years of seclusion had dampened his indignation against the world but their emotion for one another had rekindled it. He wanted to know why he wasn't the one standing in his own yard with his own family with his own smile on his own face. He wanted to know why and he knew no matter how many times he asked there would never be an answer.

That was the last thought he had as he pulled into the parking lot of the liquor store and he barely tried to talk himself out of it as he got out of the truck and pulled open the glass door and the bell jingled and the clerk said how you doing and he scanned the meager stock of the shelves and moved toward the brown liquor and took no time in grabbing a pint of Evan Williams and paying for it and returning to the truck and sitting there with it gripped in his hand like some timeless artifact and when he unscrewed the cap and turned it up it tasted so good and burned so good and his eyes watered and changed in an instant into the eyes of the wolf.

He drove to the abandoned movie theater and parked. He drank from the bottle and stared at the cracked glass of the ticket window. The faded and wrinkled movie posters in the light boxes. The blue tarp that hung over the side of the roof and the crumbling mortar of the brick wall and the words across the warped and molded marquee that read CLOSED FOR STORM. He drank and smoked and he slumped down in the seat to avoid his reflection in the rearview mirror because he didn't want to hear it. He was happy when each sip hit his lips and disgusted by the time it hit his stomach and he knew that he would simmer alone and end up smashing the truck right through the wall of the theater if he sat there much longer so he cranked the engine and drove again.

He didn't know there remained a functional bar anywhere in town but when he saw the neon in the window as he drove along the railroad tracks, he slapped his hand on the steering wheel and shouted hallelujah. Maybe there is a God. He put the cap on the whiskey and tossed it in the floorboard and he strolled toward the neon glow as if it might be the light of heaven and he stepped inside just as the last of the pallid day slipped over the edge of the horizon and dissipated into darkness.

The barroom was narrow and without windows. Yellowed and murky lamplight emanated from smokestained bulbs and a cloud of smoke hung above the heads of the handful of regulars gathered around the bar. A sagging hardwood floor. Dusty shelves and dusty liquor bottles. The stale and stagnant smell of time no more. All eyes on Wade as he pulled out a stool and nearly lost his balance as he shifted to sit down, the whiskey going down easy while he sat in the truck but catching him fast now with movement. As he gathered himself he thought someone might say something smart but the regulars disregarded him in an instant, sucking on their cigarettes and shifting their forlorn eyes back to the mirror behind the bar and the familiar reflections of surrender.

He ordered a whiskey shot for himself and the others. One of them wanted to know what they were supposed to be celebrating and he said if you can figure out what the hell there is to celebrate then you ring a bell or fire a cannon or do some shit to let us all know. This shot is for nothing but drinking. They drank and the thick bottoms of shot glasses knocked against the bar and Wade told the bartender to fill them up again. A cigarette hung from the corner of her crooked mouth and she sagged like the regulars, decades of smoke and drink and barroom darkness pulling at her eyes and earlobes and Wade smiled at her when she poured the whiskey and smiled at her when his lighter went out and she handed him a pack of matches and he found himself laughing out loud at nothing in particular as he drank and smoked with the ferocity of a man deep into a quarrel he could never win and he proclaimed to them all that the worst decision he ever made in his entire life was to quit drinking.

He didn't know who later helped him out of the bar and into the truck and he didn't know who drove him home and was kind enough to stop twice to let him puke on the side of the road. He didn't know who followed them out to his house and then drove them both away and he didn't know why they left him lying flat on his back in the dewdrenched grass but that's where he was when he awoke the next day. Flat on his back and arms outstretched and mouth open and dry. A sprinkle of rain had begun to fall across the land and the air that had been so still and stagnant the day before now began to move in a steady breeze as somewhere out across the Gulf the storm was getting stronger and moving closer. The rain dampened his face and neck and when he opened his bloodshot eyes, his thoughts were so black and confused as to where he was and what he had done that when he touched his fingers to his rainwet face he began to wonder what kind of nightmare could cause a man to cry.

40

'I THOUGHT YOU QUIT DRINKING,' Jessie said. She nudged Wade with her foot and he rolled over in the wet grass. He lifted his head and smacked his dry lips. A streak of vomit was crusted on his shirt where he had wiped his mouth. He moaned and rubbed his hand across his forehead.

She held a cup of coffee to him and he took the cup.

'What happened?' she asked.

'You're pretty much looking at it.'

'Can you get up? It's raining.'

He looked up at her with one eye closed. She wore a straw cowboy hat she had found in her old closet and the rain made tiny taps on the brim.

'I know it's raining,' he said.

'Then get up and get out of it.'

She moved beneath the cover of the porch and sat down in a chair and watched him. He sat up in the rain and sipped some of the coffee before tossing the rest and then he managed to get to his feet, the hangover driving hard through the back of his neck as he got upright.

'Jesus Christ,' he said. He wavered a moment as if to gather his equilibrium. Jessie shook her head as he moved across the yard and up the steps in slow motion, like some rusted mechanism in need of oil. He finally made it and sat down beside her, laying his head back on the chair and closing his eyes.

'You don't have time to be hungover,' she said.

He didn't answer. Didn't move.

'Do you hear me?'

He didn't answer. Didn't move.

'I know you hear me.'

'I don't have nothing but time. From this chair that's all there is.'

'Not if you're going anywhere with me. Or did you forget about that? Funny how a good drunk makes you forget.'

'I said I would go with you and the boy. I didn't say nothing about going anywhere with him.'

'Well. He is us, Wade. You should know that by now.'

He leaned his head forward and held the coffee cup to her.

'I guess you want a refill,' she said.

Wade nodded. She took the cup but she did not get up.

'I want you to do whatever you got to do to feel better. Brush your teeth. Stick your head in the shower. Swallow a dozen Tylenols. I don't care. Because me and Holt are going to sit you down and give you the whole shebang.'

'I decided I don't want to hear it.'

'When did you decide that?'

'About two steps inside the bar last night.'

They told him anyway. Sitting around the kitchen table. Jessie did most of the talking and Holt reaffirmed the things she tried to explain and sometimes made corrections where his experience with the Temple of Pain and Glory was concerned. Jace sat on her lap and played with a stack of colored blocks as she led the story right up through running through the woods with the keys and stealing the hatchback and the wolf on a chain that damn near got them. She covered Jace's ears when she whispered about the body she pulled out of the trunk and left on the side of the road and she carried the tale right up until the moment she pulled up into Wade's yard in the hatchback. When she was done, she set Jace down and he took his blocks and wandered across the room and then Holt added the details of the van and the wreck and what he had to do to survive it all.

'Whose truck is that?' Wade asked.

Holt told him about the old man who dragged him from the road and how he left him and how he tried to get the old man to come with him but he wouldn't.

The whiskey bottle from the cabinet sat on the counter from the night before. Wade got up and poured into his coffee cup.

'It's ten o'clock in the morning,' Jessie said.

He drank. Still foggy from the night before. He set the cup down and folded his arms and leaned his hip on the counter. They were quiet for a while, listening to the thrum of the rain on the roof. Wade would not look at them, his head hanging and eyes down toward the linoleum floor as if there was some infinity there he was searching into. The long minutes were broken when Holt stood and moved over to the counter and he reached around Wade and he picked up the bottle and swigged. He then set the bottle down and returned to the chair at the table.

Wade was staring at the linoleum when he said I guess the only thing I really have to say is what in God's name do you expect me to say and before you answer I would just rewind this whole thing and add that I ain't even gonna look at you Holt and get confirmation that you knew what kind of shit you were in when you drove off with my daughter and didn't bother to tell my daughter about it until you knew she wouldn't turn back and I ain't even gonna add that neither of you could figure out when Jessie was pregnant that living in rundown houses and hiding from ravenous lunatics was not the decision of the sane and beyond that I ain't even gonna ask why in the living hell are you hanging on to these keys anyway because apparently the only magical element they possess is the ability to get you killed so I say all that to say I don't know what the hell you want me to say because I'm guessing you either know all that or you shouldn't be sitting here but you should be sitting front and center the next time that hellfire revival pops up its tent so you can empty your pockets and nod your heads like the rest of the goddamn holyrolling sheep. And just let me say I don't know nothing about what helps the hunters find the hunted when they really want to find who they're looking for but I'm guessing if you had that baby in a hospital and you gave them your real names and you have to give them your real names to have a baby in a hospital then that means whoever is hunting you has your names and the name of everybody you're connected to and if your name ever beeps or pops up anywhere they know it. I've seen enough television shows to know that so besides me not saying any of that shit I just said I honest to God don't know what you want me to say.

Jessie stood and walked to the counter and she picked up the bottle and swigged and she held it to her father. He took it and did the same and then he handed it back to her and she carried it with her to the table.

'I told you he'd understand,' she said to Holt.

'I'm glad you think this is funny,' Wade answered.

'I don't think it's funny. I'm scared shitless.'

Wade picked up the coffee cup and drank again and waved it at Holt.

'And what about you? You think it's funny?'

'I ain't laughing. Am I?'

'And what about him?' Wade said and now he moved around the counter to where he could see Jace and he motioned toward him with the cup of coffee and whiskey. 'Think he'd be laughing?'

'Nobody's laughing, Wade,' Jessie said. 'Stop it.'

'Stop what? I got to start before I stop and I don't even know where to start.'

Jessie rose from her chair.

'Nobody asked you to start nothing either. We're not telling you this for you to solve it.'

'Then why are you telling me?'

'Because you're my daddy and I wish you'd act like it for once.'

'You got every right to see the craziness in it all. I see it too,' Holt said. 'There's nothing like waking up every day and thinking this could be the day you die if you take a wrong step.'

'It must not bother you too bad.'

Jessie moved to Wade and took him by the arm. His brow was bent in frustration and he would not look at her and she tugged on him.

'Look at me,' she said. Across the room Jace repeated his mother's words as he played with the blocks. With the sound of the boy's voice Wade relented. He looked at Jessie and shook his head slowly.

'We are here. And we're alive,' she said. 'I'd like to keep it that way.'

She released his arm and moved back to the table and sat down. Wade drank from the coffee cup and Holt drank from the bottle and a sudden gust of wind pushed across the land and the windows of the small house rattled.

'Where are the keys?' Wade asked.

Holt stood up and left the table and when he returned from the hallway he dropped them in the middle of the table and they hit heavy and with a clang.

'They look like they belong to a dungeon,' Wade said.

'They look like they belong to a treasure chest to me,' Jessie said. 'I think it's money.'

Holt sat back down.

'What do you think?' Wade asked him.

'I thought it was money. Now I ain't so sure.'

'How come?'

Holt's eyes seemed to sink back as if he was slipping away into a dark place. He pressed his hands together and looked at the keys and clenched his jaw as if the thought of it all was hurting him in some way. He then began to talk about the tall man with the blackrimmed glasses and how he would appear at the revival and then disappear from the revival and then Holt said sometimes he didn't seem real. When I looked at him I felt like he was aware of things no one else could know. I don't know how to explain it. Sometimes I thought he was made of shadow. Like you could walk up to him and stick your hand right through. Other times he wasn't no more to me than another soulstealing crook counting out the offering basket with Elser. Except he let her do all the work from what I could tell. He was just there. I swear he was like a shadow. And I used to catch him staring at me. I'd look up from whatever I was doing, folding chairs or loading tables or whatever and his eyes would be on me and it shook me up a little. I won't lie. He knew something. Or at least he acted like it. Only thing he ever said to me was you got scars on your soul and I didn't need to hear nothing else out of his mouth. Then I saw him and Elser passing those keys back and forth. I saw the maps with the notes and markings. It's been damn near three years since I got away from them but it feels like yesterday. I can't get his dark eyes out of my mind and I can't get those words out of my head and maybe it's money they're after but I can believe it could be anything. Or anybody. Holt slumped back in the chair. He crossed his arms and studied the keys and then he said I'm over it. I need to be over it. We both need to be over it. Holt then looked at Jessie.

It was the most Wade had ever heard him talk.

Jace was having a conversation with himself and his small voice filled the space with the words of his imagination and the rain fell harder and the smell of whiskey and coffee hung in the complicated air between them.

Wade knew why they couldn't let go. They wanted to believe that the keys opened the lock to the miracle that would change their lives and he knew no such miracle existed. There was no rising from the dead and there was no hand to calm the storms and there was no peace in no valley.

'Come on,' Wade said to Holt. 'Let's go.'

'Go where?'

'We're going to take the truck back to the old man.'

'Wade,' Jessie said.

'What?'

'What does that help?'

'It'll help me because it's something that makes sense and none of this makes sense to me. You're the ones who have been through it. You have seen the signs or whatever you want to call it. But we're taking the truck back because I can understand how to do that. And while we're taking the truck back you can figure out what you want to do next.'

'What if I don't want to do nothing.'

'You can't do nothing.'

'It's what you do.'

'Yeah. And look where it's got me.'

41

WADE DUG AROUND IN THE glovebox and found the insurance card to the truck and saw the old man's name was Oron Felder. He dug around some more and came across a receipt for new tires and his address was given in the customer information. Wade went back inside the house and told them it wasn't far. Maybe a dozen miles. Maybe fifteen. He told Holt to follow him and he gave him the keys to his own truck and they drove off into the rain with Jessie standing on the porch and holding Jace as they watched the red taillights disappear down the slippery crop road.

The steady rain of the gray world as they wound the empty roads toward the old man's property. Wade took a wrong turn at a four-way stop and they wheeled around in the parking lot of a yellowbrick church where plywood covered cracked stainedglass windows and the steeple shook in the wind. Soggy haybales lay scattered in the rolling fields and a deer darted across the road and leapt the fence in a graceful spring and Wade sat forward in the seat with both hands on the steering wheel. The rain slackened as he drove on and there was a break as he began to slow, approaching what he believed to be the right place.

He saw the skid marks first and then the small mound lying in the road. He slowed and rolled down his window, leaning his head out and seeing the coyote, eyes stuck open and its hind legs pecked at by vultures. Past the coyote he saw the mailbox for Oron Felder at the edge of the gravel driveway and beyond that were two more mounds lying just off the road. Wade pulled close and stopped the truck and looked at the slumped bodies. The bloodstained trail from the asphalt to where they lay. Holt parked behind him and got out and he walked up to Wade's door and in that instant the story became real to Wade in a way that was not possible as they were sitting at the kitchen table.

'The van was right there,' Holt said. He pointed to the spot in the ditch where it had been, the weeds depressed and tire marks dug in the dirt.

'So somebody came and got the van but not the bodies.'

'Looks like it.'

'And that's the old man's driveway over there?'

Holt looked over his shoulder and nodded. He then returned to Wade's truck. They both backed the vehicles away from the dead men and then began along the driveway toward Oron's house. Rocking and splashing over the uneven gravel.

The old man was lying on his side in the middle of the yard. Tire marks crisscrossed the property as if some game of chase had been played around the corpse. The front door of the house was open and the rockers of the porch overturned. Both trucks parked. Holt got out first and he was carrying the shotgun. Wade followed and walked behind him and they stopped at the body of the old man. His finger was still wrapped around the trigger of the pistol and he lay as if he was not only dead but also broken, the awkward pose of care no more. His hair was matted against his head with rain and blood and a dark mudpuddle had begun to form beneath his cheek that pressed into the earth.

'Shit,' Holt said. He looked up from the old man and around the place. 'I asked him to come with me.'

Wade moved away. He looked into the open door of the house and furniture was toppled and the litter of a house ransacked covered the floor. He then returned to Oron's truck and he reached in and took the keys from the ignition. He crossed the yard to the porch steps and he tossed the keys into the open doorway and they hit and slid across the floor.

'What are you doing that for?' Holt asked.

'It's not my truck. Is it yours?'

'It might be helpful if we all load up and leave.'

'I didn't realize you had a bunch of shit you had to load up.'

Wade pulled cigarettes from his pocket and he lit one. A soft rain began to fall. Thunder echoed in the southern sky and deeper shades of gray had begun to paint the horizon. Wade smoked and walked across the yard and to the barn. He looked in and saw the Buick and then he turned around and stood with Holt who was still standing next to the old man. He held the shotgun barrel propped on his shoulder.

'You ever heard of a place called the Bottom?' Holt asked.

'No.'

'You sure?'

'It don't sound like something you'd forget,' Wade said.

'I think it's not far from here.'

'Does that mean a mile or twenty miles or fifty miles?'

'I don't know.'

'What's it supposed to be?'

'When I was in the back of the van that's where they said we were going.'

'I never heard of it,' Wade said. He tossed the cigarette away and took one more long look at the old man and then he told Holt to get in the truck. We don't need to be here.

They climbed in and Wade lit another cigarette and gave one to Holt. The shotgun leaned against Holt's leg and Wade poked the barrel.

'You have to carry that thing around?'

'What else do you need to see?' Holt said. He grabbed a lighter from the bench seat and lit his cigarette. 'Besides. You got a few. I've seen them in this very truck.'

'Not anymore.'

'Stolen?'

'Nah. Drank them.'

'Drank them?'

'Took them to the pawn shop. Got some money. Drank them. Just as well anyhow.'

'How so?'

He thought to say I didn't need a gun lying around. The nights had started to get harder and I was afraid I might eat the end of a barrel in the middle of one of those nights when the wind seemed like it might lift me and the house and everything and carry us off. Or in the middle of one of those nights where there was no sound but silence and those were worse. So I got rid of them. Drinking was safer. At least for a while. But he didn't say any of that.

'Nevermind,' Wade said.

'You think they're close?' Holt asked.

'You mean whoever did this? Whoever had you and whoever dragged off the van and left their dead right where they are? You mean those people?'

Holt didn't answer. He drew on the cigarette. The rain streaked the windshield and gave them a wavy view of the old man and his place.

'I swear I asked him to come with me,' Holt said.

'You should have told him.'

When they returned to the house Wade and Holt got out and walked through the rain and toward the porch. Jessie was sitting there reading to Jace while the boy nibbled on the corner of a cracker. She looked up as they climbed the steps.

'You get it back to him?' she said.

'Kind of,' Wade answered. 'He wasn't there anymore.'

'You just left it?'

Holt made a pistol with his hand and he raised it to his head and mimicked the gunshot.

'I'm going to the sheriff,' Wade said.

'What for?' Holt said.

'Are you being serious?'

'That ain't smart.'

'Like anything you've done up to this very instant is smart.'

'You know how law is down here now. What little there is you damn sure can't trust.'

'I don't know what the law is like and what's more I don't give a shit. That old man is laying out there and he needs to be buried and his place needs to be taken care of and for that to happen it has to be reported.'

Holt looked at Jessie.

'Would you tell him?' he said.

She shook her head.

Holt huffed and went inside the house. Jace wiggled down from Jessie's lap and followed Holt. Jessie stood and stretched her arms over her head. She had slept better in the last two days than she had in the last two years but she still looked tired. Her eyes seemed set in some faraway gaze no matter what she was looking at and she stood with her shoulders leaned forward like she had when she was a child and her school backpack was much too big for her small frame.

She walked to the edge of the porch and held her hand out under the runoff from the roof. She then touched her rainwet fingers to her cheeks. She closed her eyes and touched her eyelids. Then she set her hands on the porchrail and looked out at the weather and in her profile Wade could only see her mother.

'Where do you think she went?' she asked. As if she could see his thoughts.

Wade folded his arms. He took a couple of steps closer to her. Looked out at the space above the cornstalks where her eyes held fixed on the endless gray.

'Heaven?' she said.

He had stared into the same space above the same corn on many days and many nights. Standing in the same spot. His hands propped on the same porchrail. His thoughts filled with the same questions.

'Is there such a place?' he said.

'I think so. If for no other reason than I like to imagine her being somewhere special like that. I like to imagine there would be that sort of place for Jace one day.'

The sky brightened in flashes of silent lightning. Wade took another step closer to her. For so long he had only thought of her as a girl but she was beyond that. And he had missed it. He had let her childhood slip right past him and now she was another person. A protector and a provider. He remembered night after night after night of his own questions when she lay in her childhood room, crying and fussing in her own little furies against the world and all he had were questions about what to do and how to do it and what the hell happened and how did I get here and on and on and the questions never stopped. They had paused in the last years of being alone as he tried to make peace with it all. With his failures as a father and as a man and he instead spent his time trying to reconcile his newfound sobriety and how he would keep it together as a citizen of the stormravaged region and it was in his own solitude that he found the answer. Stay alone. Stay far away from anyone and anything. Hunker down. And your eyes will remain clear.

But now he was hungover. And his eyes were not clear. And he was not alone. He moved another step toward her until he was standing right beside Jessie. Their shoulders nearly touching. Their eyes into the same sky with the same questions.

'Heaven,' she said. 'It's pretty in my mind.'

'How's it look in your mind?'

She tilted her head to the side as if to see better. She thought a moment and then she waved her hand like some magician preparing to create the illusion.

'I don't see big clouds and angels and golden gates and all that stuff you hear people say. I think it looks a lot like this. Except it's green all the time. The weather is good. Everybody is safe and everybody gets along.'

It surprised him. But she could see it. And so could he.

'Do you think that's where she went?'

She turned to him then and it struck him how big the world was inside her eyes.

'Yeah,' he said. 'That's what I think.'

The door opened and Jace poked his head out. He was wearing the straw cowboy hat and it fell down over his eyes and he held his arms out, feeling his way.

'Come on, cowboy,' Jessie said and she reached down and scooped him up.

'I'm going to report the old man and then when I get back, let's get the hell out of here.'

'You sure?' she asked.

'You drive your little borrowed hatchback and I'll hook up the trailer to the truck. I can make a delivery and get us a little more money than I got already and we'll just go until you think it's safe. I'll let you tell him.'

'Tell him what?' Holt said. He stood in the doorway.

'That it's time to go,' Jessie said.

42

THE RAGGEDY BLACK HEARSE WAS parked and running, a plume of blue smoke from the tailpipe as the rough engine chugged. Elser sat in a cloud of cigarette smoke and watched it rain as she waited for the tall man to join her on the top level of the three-tier parking garage. She sat facing the bridge that crossed from downtown into East McComb. She expected there to be more of a moving about with the evacuation order and the hours dwindling until the hurricane arrived but the streets were quiet with only the random vehicle crossing the bridge. The revival had praised God and sung hallelujah only weeks before from the very spot where the hearse was now parked, using the elevation of the parking garage as proof of the revival's commitment to reaching as close to heaven as it could possibly reach.

The hearse now bore fresh messages of condemnation, written by Elser in white spraypaint in a moment of boredom that led to inspiration. Along the length of the driver's side it read YOU DROVE THE NAILS. Along the passenger's side it read YOU SPILLED THE BLOOD. The messages were sloppy but clear.

A motorcycle crossed the bridge. The rider wearing a black helmet with a black facemask and covered from head to toe in rain gear. Elser opened the door of the hearse and was waving the smoke out into the rain when the murmur of the motorcycle began to rise up the ramp of the parking garage. She closed the door of the hearse and was reaching beneath the seat for a pistol when the motorcycle hit the brake, sliding on the wet pavement and fishtailing right up to Elser's door. With a gloved hand the rider tapped on the window.

She rolled it down a couple of inches.

'Go to the sheriff's department at the county line,' the voice said from behind the mask. 'They got the info you need.'

'Where is he?'

'He sent me to tell you what I told you. That's all I know. And he said you'd better hurry.'

'Why?'

'Because he's waiting for you. He's waiting to show you what you've been looking for.'

The sheriff's department sat back off the road on a wide stretch of asphalt. The department was shared by Pike and Walthall counties as numbers and funding had dwindled across south Mississippi and sheriff and fire and rescue departments doubled and sometimes tripled up. In the parking lot to one side of the office building there was a gathering of storage trucks with FEMA stenciled on the sides. Behind the office building stood a windowless cinderblock building and stretching out from the building was a great rectangle of chainlink fence with a large and looping coil of barbed wire reaching across the top of the fence. Very young men and very old men and all ages in between milled around inside the rectangle in orange jumpsuits and tried to smoke cigarettes in the rain. Around the edges of the property rows of pine trees stood in parallel lines like good soldiers awaiting the call.

Wade pulled into the parking lot. He parked at the edge, away from the cruisers and away from what looked like a family hugging and crying in a moment of heartbreak. He killed the engine. The lights from the front windows of the office building gave squares of light against the deepening sky.

He wanted to make this quick but wasn't sure how that was going to happen. He wished he could write down the name of the old man and his address and what had happened on a slip of paper and drop it in a mail slot and sneak away. Instead he got out of the truck, resigned to do what he felt he had to do and he even questioned that now.

What difference does it make?

Just shut up and do it.

He walked between cars, watching teenage boys load boxes into the back of a FEMA truck and then shifting his eyes to the men in orange jumpsuits and a ruckus that was breaking out in the corner of the chainlink rectangle. He heard the hearse before he saw the hearse. Like some intrusive and foulrunning proclamation. He turned toward the chugging as the big and awkward vehicle slowed on the highway and then turned into the parking lot. It sputtered and smoked and eased around the parked vehicles and came to a stop at the side of the building. The words across the side of the hearse screamed at him.

YOU SPILLED THE BLOOD

Wade froze. The vehicle sat chugging and then the door opened with a metal groan. The old prophet got out and looked around. Her piercing eyes and hellbent brow and she caught Wade looking at her and she returned his stare until he shrunk away and took two steps backward as the Temple of Pain and Glory came to life in the bawdy figure of what Wade knew could only be its leader as she moved with the certainty and deadpan stare that Holt had described in a shaken voice.

She walked around the hearse and was pulling open the door of the sheriff's department when Wade turned and ran back to his truck. He cranked it and spun out of the parking lot and spun onto the highway back toward a home he knew they should have already left. The driving was slow and aggravating as he got stuck behind evacuating families piled into cars and big trucks staying off the interstate because of the clutter and the rain fell in gray sheets and he banged the steering wheel. Frustrated and scared now and talking to himself and the words along the hearse repeating in his head. You spilled the blood you spilled the blood. It took way too long for him to manipulate the cars and rigs along the thin highway but when he made a right at the crossroads that led him toward home he began to relent, believing he would make it to them and they would make it away and tonight they would be somewhere else.

He turned onto the crop road and the stalks slumped with the rain. The road had turned slick and gathered the water and he saw the sloppy tire tracks that sunk and cut across the blackdirt road from one side to the other and there was no mistaking the tracks belonged to more than one vehicle and the vehicles had been in a rush.

The first thing he saw when he came to the end of the crop road was the windows of the hatchback shot out. The second thing he saw was a man lying facedown beside it. He rolled up into the yard and slammed the brakes, tires locking and sliding across the wet grass. Inside the truck he reached for guns that were no longer there and then he pulled a tire iron from beneath the seat and he got out and squatted behind the open truck door. He watched for the man to move but he was dead. He listened for voices but there was only the drone of the storm.

The front door was open. Shotgun blasts splintered the wooden slats of the house. Splintered one of the porch posts. A hole was blown through the screen and glass of a window.

'Jessie!' he yelled.

He waited. Then he called out again before he began mumbling to himself in a ramble of profanity and desperation. Godfuckingdamnshit. Please God. Please God. Fuckinggoshdamnfuck please no. He climbed the steps of the porch mumbling and cussing and praying and he went inside and the couch and its cushions had been ripped open with a blade and the stuffing lay about like wasted clumps of cotton. The television screen had been shot. The kitchen table had been overturned and had been used for protection as the round top was pocked with buckshot. The whiskey bottle and coffee cups were scattered on the floor and a trail of blood lay across the linoleum floor.

'Jessie!'

He dropped the tire iron and stepped into the hallway.

'Jessie. Jace? Jace?'

In both bedrooms the mattresses had been stripped of their sheets and slit with knives and dresser drawers were spilled onto the floor and it seemed as if he had been gone for days and not an hour. It seemed as if he had left one life and returned to another and he knew that feeling and he dropped to the floor in the hallway and disappeared down into that known darkness. He sat there lifeless. Barely breathing. And then he called out again in a feeble and broken voice.

'Jessie. Jace.'

The knock came from his bedroom. Delicate. He raised his head, trying to decide if he had heard something or not.

Another bump. He crawled over to the open door of his bedroom and looked in. Nothing moved.

He waited.

From the back of the closet the knock came again. Wade got to his feet and stepped across the mattress and emptied drawers. The closet door was wedged closed with the fallen dresser and he moved it and opened the door and in the back of the closet the box shifted with the movement of the hidden child. Wade opened the box flap and Jace reached out and pointed his tiny finger at Wade.

'Wade,' he said.

'My God,' Wade said and he lifted Jace out of the box. He hugged the boy. Squeezed him. And then Wade began to break into pieces as he kept repeating I can't believe it before he broke into the gasping and breathless cry of the astounded.

43

WADE TRIED TO GET JACE to tell him anything. And the boy worked hard to explain. He pointed and made motions with his hands and said words like momma and da and bang and hide. He told Wade it's dark and he told Wade momma come back and the toddler seemed unfazed by the spectacle as if he was perfectly at ease in the violence that surrounded him.

Wade searched through the wreckage but there was nothing to find, only the trashstrewn relics of this thing he had called life. He knew the keys were gone but he looked anyway and then he stuffed some of Jace's clothes and diapers into a plastic bag and he picked him up and carried him out to the truck. He sat behind the wheel and stared at the house. He could not go to the sheriff's office because Elser had gone to the sheriff's office and that was that.

The Bottom, he thought.

He cranked the truck and pulled around to the back of the house. He left Jace in the cab while he hooked up the cattle trailer filled with the HVAC units and scrap and then he hustled back behind the wheel. He then held Jace in his lap as he drove the crop row and the boy reached his small hands and touched the steering wheel as if helping. Wade watched the house shrink in the rearview mirror and he tried to remember this land in the sunshine and he tried to remember her sitting on the porch and painting her toenails with her belly growing and he tried to remember the cornstalks being tall and green and he tried to remember anything that hadn't faded in the muted tones of storm and solitude and none of it would come.

He stopped in front of the mobile home and honked the horn. A rusted sheetmetal awning hung across a makeshift deck and a brown dog raised its head from slumber at the sound. The dog stared for a moment and laid its head back down and Wade honked the horn again. The mobile home was surrounded with a clutter of automobiles in various states of repair and he expected Alvin to slip out from under a raised hood with a socket wrench in one hand and a tallboy in the other but he was nowhere to be found. A soft rain continued and the wind rocked the seats of a swingset that nestled between a Cadillac on blocks and a Jeep without a top.

'Come on, Jace,' Wade said. He opened the door and climbed out. He carried Jace and the plastic bag with his clothes and diapers and stepped around machine parts and hubcaps on his way toward the deck. The dog raised its head and gave a lazy yowl of alarm and then the front door opened and Alvin appeared. A young girl peeked her head around his hip.

'Where's Melissa?' Wade said.

'Huh?'

'Melissa. She here?'

'Yeah. Come on out of the rain.'

'Go get her,' Wade said. He came up the deck stairs and stepped over the dog and stood beneath the awning. Alvin's long beard reached the collar of his flannel shirt and he raised his hand and scratched somewhere inside the whiskers.

'What you got there?'

'Goddamn it. I said get Melissa. Can you hear?'

'Fine. Shit,' Alvin said. He nudged the girl and told her to go and get momma and she slipped back out of sight.

'What's that?' he asked and he pointed at Jace.

'It's my grandson.'

'What?'

'I swear to God, Alvin. You heard me.'

'I know I hear you but – '

He was interrupted when Melissa sidled up next to him.

'What's that?' she said.

Wade turned and pointed at the trailer being pulled by his truck.

'You see all that? It's yours. All you got to do is take it to that junkyard off the interstate up around South Jackson. Back off the exit behind that porn store. You know it?'

Alvin looked down at Melissa and then back at Wade. Three pigtailed heads had followed their mother to see what was going on.

'I didn't mean you go to the porn store I meant you know where it is. You do?'

'Yeah.'

'Drive it up there to the junkyard beside it and they'll give you a nice price for it all. Better payday than you've had since God knows when. But you got to help me.'

Melissa edged around Alvin. A shawl was wrapped around her shoulders and her hair was gathered in a long braid. She reached out to Jace and he wrapped his fingers around her thumb.

'We got enough already,' Alvin said.

'Hush,' Melissa snapped.

'It's not forever. It's just for a little while. I can't explain it all I just need some help and you think I'd have more options but I don't.'

'This Jessie's baby?' Melissa said.

'Yes.'

'Where is she?'

'Can you take him for a little while? I'm begging but I'm also kind of saying you got to.'

Melissa held out her hands and Wade handed him over to her. She then looked back at Wade and recognized the despair on his face. She and Alvin had been there when he brought Jessie home from the hospital, newly widowed and holding the tiny thing that he had no idea what to do with. And they had been there two days later when they put Rebecca in the ground and she knew by his expression that whatever was going on was bad.

'What's his name?' she said.

'Jace.'

He handed the plastic bag to Alvin.

'You are coming back,' he said. 'Ain't you?'

'Are you staying through the hurricane?'

'Maybe. We still got a day to decide.'

Alvin leaned out and pointed at the cable wire tied to the corners of the mobile home that were stretched taut and held by spikes driven into the ground or tied to discarded car engines.

'You got four kids out here. Don't be stupid,' Wade said.

'You never run off from one.'

'Yeah. Well. There's a lot of shit I should've done that I didn't.'

Wade shook his head. Then he reached out and touched the

soft hair of the back of Jace's head and he started to promise the boy that he would be back but he stopped himself. He wanted to tell him he would be back or his momma would be back or anything that might make this moment more promising but instead he told Alvin and Melissa thanks and he turned and walked back out into the rain, ignoring Alvin when he said we really do have more than we can handle.

44

THERE WAS ONE LAST STOP to make. He pushed the truck hard through the rainstorm and hydroplaned twice in low stretches of road but he held it together and stayed between the ditches. He smoked aggressively. He cussed the world. He wanted to believe that Jessie was alive. He even wanted to believe that Holt was alive. The stormclouds smothered the sky and the palegray light began to fade and the landscape became saturated in darkness.

He returned to the old man's place and the rain slashed across the headlights as he moved between the fields and approached the house. He parked and sat there and watched but this was the home of the dead where nothing moved or spoke. The old man lay there in the rain, illuminated by the headlights that in some biblical scenario may have been the lights of heaven readying to lift and carry him toward paradise.

Wade got out of the truck and he hurried across the yard and into the house. He flipped on the lights and it had been wrecked just like Wade's, furniture tossed and ripped open and closets and drawers spilled out. He went into the kitchen and opened cabinet doors until he found what he was looking for. A nearly empty fifth of rye but it would have to do. He held the bottle by the neck and he returned to the living room where he found a blanket wadded on the floor. He turned off the lights. Closed the door behind him. And then he walked back to the old man and he knelt beside him. A grotesque figure in a lost and sodden night. He set the bottle down and then he spread the blanket across Oron Felder's body. Wade dropped his head a moment as if to offer some prayer and then he turned up the bottle and drank. He looked up at his truck and the headlights stared back at him and the rain was going to keep on coming down and he had told Holt that he had never heard of the Bottom but that had been a lie. He did not know if that's where his daughter had been taken and he did not know if he could find it and he did not even know if it was real but in a world of questions the possibility of the Bottom was the only answer. He reached down and removed the pistol from the old man's rigid fingers and then he climbed in the truck and drove off into the night.

IV

IV

45

IT HAD BEEN THE PREFERRED method of killing time when Wade was young and his friends were young and they didn't have a damn thing to do other than load a cooler with beer and ice and ride the dark and snaking backroads underneath the widereaching skies that draped the Mississippi and Louisiana line. They rode off into dense stretches of forest where dirt roads trailed down into the belly of nowhere, where things howled and screeched hidden in the great depths of black. They followed unknown roads of rough asphalt marked with spraypainted or gunshot roadsigns, unknown roads they never found again. They rode between the acres and acres of farmland where on summer nights the moon hung in the indigo sky like the watchful eye of some benevolent god. And they rode the lowlying routes through the swamplands where the cypress knots reached up from the blackwater like arms outstretched in the final and desperate grasp for salvation.

They rode in all directions and covered as much distance as the gas in the tank would allow them to cover and they sometimes had girls with them and most of the time they only wished they had girls with them. They told lies and talked of things that burgeoning men would not talk about in the light of day or without the truth serum of several beers and they swapped the stories they had heard from those who had driven these roads before them about this place called the Bottom and when the subject turned to the legend, they swore that they would be the ones to finally find it during one of their nightlong journeys beyond the pale.

The Bottom was out there. They were sure of this. And the tales that they had heard about the mythical place had no limit. Maybe it was in Mississippi and maybe it was in Louisiana. It was somewhere that did not exist on a map. It was somewhere that was lost in time. A place to be reckoned with. It was a haunted and ghoulish settlement of old graves that had been pushed to the surface from a hundred years of flooding and the caskets lay broken and open as the dead walked in the night looking for a dry place to rest. It was a last retreat for Confederate soldiers during the Civil War where the men grew so hungry and frail that a horde of alligators watched from surrounding marshes and then feasted on the feeble soldiers too weakened to escape. It was a fortress created by pirates where cannons poked between thickets of twisted vines and booby traps capable of decapitation protected the mounds of treasure hidden in its rotted depths. It was an insane asylum where the tortured cries of the demented patients could be heard echoing through the midnight fog. It was a home for devil worshipers gathered to make sacrifice to their heathen god and drink the blood of the innocent. It was inhabited by sex cults where mobs of the naked and the carnal sang to one another in the moaning and groaning of copulation. The Bottom had many lives and many truths, depending on the generation and the kinfolk of the storyteller but the one thing that all of the stories agreed upon was that the entrance to the Bottom was marked by a thick stone wall and an ancient gate decorated with a cross that may or may not have been upside down. Nobody was sure how this was known about a place none of them had ever seen.

Wade had not thought of any of this in thirty years. Now he thought of it all as he filled his truck with gas. The fluorescent lights hummed above his head as he held the nozzle with one hand and smoked with the other. The gas station sat alone somewhere down into the Louisiana countryside as he was heading southeast. His mind filled with the blackest of roads and the rich and heavy growth of a natural world that hid the Bottom from them. There was no way that was the word Holt had used. No goddamn way. But it was. No matter how hard he tried to hear the question in a different way, it came back the same each time.

You ever heard of a place called the Bottom?

He returned the nozzle to the pump and he went inside. He grabbed a few bags of chips and some beer and cigarettes. He picked up a roadmap and a flashlight. He paid for it all and returned to the truck. He pulled out from the station and back into the rhythm of the rain and the slosh of the road. There was only rain now but tomorrow there would be rain and wind and the next day worse rain and wind and how bad and for how long there was no way to tell.

The single memory burned behind his eyes as he drove through the dark. It had been the one and only time he had taken Jessie on any kind of vacation as a child. She was four years old and the summer had been a stretch of drought. He had bought a round plastic pool and filled it with the water hose and she would splash around in her little yellow bikini as he watched her from the cover of a shade tree. Hot beneath the shade and hot everywhere and he had finished the beer he was drinking and without saying a word to her he got up and went inside and packed a bag for both of them and then he locked the house and walked out and set the bag in the truck. He picked up the towel that lay on the ground next to the pool and he lifted her out of the water and wrapped her in the towel and he carried her to the truck and as he buckled her in he said if you want to play in the water I think you should play in the big water.

An hour and a half later the truck pulled into the parking lot of the Seaside Motel in Bay St. Louis. White stucco and skyblue shutters and a swimming pool. Pink flamingos in the flower bed in front of the motel office. A short walk to the beach. Wade got a room and Jessie had never been in a motel room before and she came alive, jumping from one bed to the other and picking up the telephone and pushing buttons and unwrapping the plastic cups next to the sink and asking what they were for. Wade stood in the breezeway and smoked and let her ramble on until she finally came out of the room and said she was ready.

'For what?' he asked her.

'The big water.'

Wade loaded three beers and ice into the room's ice bucket and they grabbed towels and walked past another motel and a crab shack before crossing the four lanes of a main drag and then stepping into the sand. Jessie came right out of her flipflops and she ran for the ocean. Wade found a spot to spread out towels between the other beachgoers. The water was calm with the lazy flop of the occasional whitecap and she ran in and out, laughing and throwing her arms and kicking her feet and the day seemed to stretch out into the reaches of a dream where life rests just on the edges of what you want it to be. The blue sky and the flakes of clouds and the sun sliding toward the horizon with patience. He finished the beers and gave her the ice bucket and they knelt together and used it to form sandcastles. A little girl about Jessie's age joined them and asked if she could help and Wade waited a moment before letting them have it and he returned to his towel and sat watching Jessie and he promised himself that he would do more. Be better. The girls built sandcastles and then used the ice bucket to gather seashells and a dead crab washed up on the shore and they studied it and then dropped it into the bucket and Wade watched the afternoon fade toward dusk. The same dusk of home. The dusk that arrived with its melancholy. He lay back on the blanket and listened to the cars passing on the main drag and the wash of the ocean and the voices of children.

At sunset they walked to the crab shack and ate boiled shrimp and corn on the cob while sitting at a wooden picnic table. Wade drank cold bottles of beer and Jessie explained everything she had figured out about sand and waves and seagulls and saltwater. The ice bucket sat beside her, holding the seashells but Wade had made her get rid of the lifeless crab. When they were done they returned to the motel. She took a bath and then lay on the bed and watched television while Wade pulled a chair outside the room. He smoked and watched twin boys play in the pool and he watched their mother with her tanned legs stretched out in the lounge chair. A small cooler beside her. Whenever she reached into the cooler for another beer she always raised it to offer Wade and he shook his head until she stopped offering. And then he really wanted one and he really wanted to go and talk to her but it was too late. Night slipped over the Gulf and she finished what was in the cooler and she stood up with a wobble and turned and grinned at Wade before calling the boys out of the pool and heading for their room.

He leaned his head into the open doorway and Jessie was asleep. Her nose and cheeks brushed with sunburn. Her arms limp by her sides. Happily exhausted.

He had never understood why he couldn't make it through that night. Why he couldn't have just crawled into the other bed and found a baseball game or rerun to watch on television and let Jessie sleep until she wanted to wake up the next morning and then go back to the beach and build more sandcastles and eat more shrimp and maybe go over to the woman at the pool and drink one of the beers from her cooler and see if her legs were as slick and tan close up as they seemed from his chair outside the room. He had never understood why he grew so restless that he paced the breezeway while Jessie slept, pacing until the woman from the motel office came out and asked him what he was doing. Nothing. I'm not doing nothing. But it was over then and he knew it. He could not define what made him do it but he returned to the room and he packed the bag and took it to the truck and then he came back and he slid his arms under his daughter and he carried her to the truck and laid her still sleeping body across the bench seat, sticking a motel pillow under her head and covering her with a motel blanket and then dropping the key to the room in the slot of the office door. He hustled to the gas station across the street from the motel, grabbing a sixpack and hurrying back but Jessie was out and she was going to stay out and he cranked the truck and opened a beer. There was a gnawing inside that he could not ignore and as he drove away from the lights of the coast he could not find a reason to explain anything he was doing and he knew that the darker the highway, the more hidden he would feel from his own unnameable angst.

When he reached Slidell he turned off of I-10 and drove north, disappearing into the Pearl River Valley. He drove on lightless county roads where the night fell in black walls and the trees gathered in mobs of green. Kudzu blanketed fence rows and wrapped utility poles and utility lines and dots of predatory eyes flashed from clumps of undergrowth. He crossed aged wooden bridges where the planks slapped with the passing of weight, bridges that stretched across river veins and abandoned rail lines and he tossed beer cans out of the window and smoked and hummed along to songs inside his head. Jessie slept hard as the truck moved over the roughworn terrain and shifted through unexpected turns when the blackroad bent into shadows before his beerlazy eyes could gather the change in direction. He slowed then, after nearly making it into two different ditches. Realizing that he was nowhere and there was nobody. The pit of night that was no place to find yourself sideways. When he came to an unmarked crossing he looked left and he looked right and he looked straight ahead and tried to recall what turns he had made but there was no use. He was lost. And the spot where the truck sat idling was on the last of the asphalt. If he did anything but turn around he would have to navigate unpaved roads. He leaned forward and looked up through the windshield for the moon. It was a wobbly globe of light that offered no answer.

He turned to the left.

In less than a mile the road shrunk down to the width of one vehicle. The weighted limbs hung low and formed a black tunnel that seemed to suck away the headlights. He drove on slowly for several miles, looking for a place to try and turn around but there was only the closing in of the natural world. The terrain turned soft then. The road ascended just enough for passage through the wetlands as the moon shifted between the willows and cypress and silver slants of lights streaked across the swampwater and he began to imagine things moving in the dark. Shadows sliding through the water. Shadows perched on the rotting trunks of fallen trees. Shadows kneeling by the roadside. Shadows watching him. He was readying to stop and shift into reverse and back out however many miles he had driven in when stretches of dry ground reappeared and the headlights showed a higher rise. He continued on, hoping that over this hill there may be another crossing or a clearing with enough hard ground to turn around or anything that would make this seem like less of a bad decision.

As the truck climbed the overgrowth grew thicker and knocked against the hood and windshield and doors and Jessie woke up and lifted her head. Sleepy and confused and Wade did not notice her as he squeezed the steering wheel and leaned forward as if to give momentum to the plunge through the darkness and then the truck reached the top of the hill and for a moment it seemed as if it may run over the edge of the earth before it began its descent and the road simply disappeared into the wild.

Wade slammed the brakes before barreling into the growth and Jessie toppled into the floorboard with a scream. She knocked her head against the glovebox and Wade shifted into park. He helped her up from the floorboard and apologized and said tell me where it hurts and she rubbed at the side of her head where a small knot was beginning to rise. She was okay until she looked around and realized they seemed to be stranded in the middle of some nightmare and then she began to cry. She began to cry and she wanted to know where they were and why they were there and when did they leave the motel and why did they leave the motel and she was scared and confused and Wade scooted across the bench seat and wrapped his arms around her.

Trying to calm her and trying to answer her questions in a way that would ease both her fear and his fear and they sat there together in such depths of darkness he did not know existed.

When she seemed like she might be okay he told her he was going to get out and look around. Just to see if it was going to be possible to back up and over the hill and he told her not to worry because they would keep backing up until they were all the way back to a real road. And they might even set a record for driving in reverse so she was going to have to help him pay attention and keep track of the distance. He tried to make a game of it all and she eased some and agreed to let him step out of the truck.

Wade pushed open the truck door, the brush and limbs pressing and scratching against it as he shoved. The headlights illuminated the lost world and gave waves of light and shadow through the dense growth. He moved along the side of the truck, pushing away limbs and vines and in the red glow of the taillights he tried to make out if what was left of the road would hold or if the tires would spin at the incline. He turned and looked back and Jessie was on her knees in the seat and watching him with her hands pressed against the back window. He raised his thumb and said it's okay. He walked a dozen feet away from the truck, trying to gauge the path and he believed they could make it though there was no choice but to try.

He walked back around the side of the truck and was about to climb in when a strange cry came from somewhere in the distance out in front of him. He was not certain how far away but the sound was perceptible. Shrill and winding. He stood at the open door and looked out into the spread of the headlights and then it came again and he told himself it can only be an animal but he could not avoid the thought that it was not an animal.

'Daddy?'

'Shhhh.'

Wade stood there watching and listening and it seemed as if creation had paused. All had gone still and quiet. No frogs or nightbirds or owls. And then he felt the strength of the moment. Something different crawled inside of him as he listened for the cry, imagining the sound to be a voice calling from some deep and desperate tunnel or hollow or empty space in the earth. He joined the stillness of the dark as he waited and felt the pull of another realm as if he had arrived at the one spot in space and time where it was possible to reach and connect to the other side. And he believed if he looked hard enough that he would be able to see Rebecca. He leaned inside the truck and flipped the headlights on bright and the light reached higher and wider. And in the extension of light he could now see that the land fell in a steady slope and deep into the trees he saw a clearing and a pathway and at the end of the pathway he saw an iron gate and the iron gate joined high and vinedraped walls.

The cry came again and he would never understand if what he saw next was real or if it had been triggered by his imagination or by his distress or by the closet in his mind that was filled with the haunted tales of his youth but a black and shapeless figure passed behind the gate. A soundless gasp and then he climbed in the truck and he dimmed the lights. Jessie was saying what is it what is it. But he wasn't listening to her. He shifted the truck into reverse and backed up the incline, the reaches of green grabbing at the truck as if trying to pull it back and the tires spun in the dirt but the truck made it up and over the hill and Wade did not stop and he told Jessie to start counting and she started counting and neither of them knew what she was supposed to be counting but by the time they had reversed all the way back to the crossing and the paved road she had counted to 527.

Now Wade sat parked at a flashing red light in a community made up of six buildings. No lights on inside. No vehicles around any of them. The flashing red like some absurd pulse. He was on the edge of the Pearl River Valley and he wondered what roads and bridges may not be there that once were. Eighteen years and twice that many hurricanes since the night he and Jessie had gotten lost. A government sign on a metal post read DO NOT STOP FOR STRANGERS. A homemade sign on a wooden post read REPENT. The windshield wipers knocked in a steady beat and he was smoking and listening to the rain. Remembering the night so long ago. Trying to remember how in the hell he got to wherever the hell they were but he knew he had seen the Bottom. And if that was where Jessie had been taken, he had to find it. He reached over and picked up the pistol and turned it in his hand and then he picked up the bottle of rye and he took a drink. Help me, he whispered. Somebody help me.

46

JESSIE SAT ON A WET concrete floor with her back against the wall. Her wrists taped together in front of her. A cloth sack over her head pulled tight and knotted with a drawstring and the last words she was told were if we come back and this sack is off or if you're so much as trying to untie the string we will choke you dead. A test they seemed to know she would fail.

A foul smell rose from the floor. The wall that she leaned on was made of brick. There was a great darkness behind the hood, a great darkness she knew existed even if the covering wasn't there. The sacks had been put over their heads when they had been shoved into the back of a vehicle and she had listened to Holt tell them you have the keys now. Let her go. She don't have nothing to do with any of this. And then she had listened to them come across the seats and beat him in the head and face. She had listened to him take it and then say it all again with his mouth filled with blood and then they came across the seats and drove fists into him until he fell over. Slumped against her. His shirt soaked where he had been shot. No longer talking but wheezing and then not wheezing. Only unmoving and quiet. We ain't supposed to kill him, one of the voices said. He ain't dead, another said. Not like he's gonna wish he was. What about her, one of them asked. You know about her, another answered. Same as the rest.

The vehicle drove on and the men talked no more and Holt never moved or said another word. When the vehicle stopped she had been separated from Holt and she had been walked through the rain and along a soggy pathway and then there was the slide of a heavy door and winding stairs. She was walked through tunnels and she had heard the clanking of iron bars and heard the rattle of keys and heard the echoes of indistinct voices and then she was left alone. Or she thought she was alone. There could have been others there who were also blind to whatever was happening. There could have been someone there watching her. Waiting for her to untie the knot and remove the sack and look around, just so he could do what had been promised.

She started to cry and when no one responded to her she believed she was unaccompanied in her despair. So she cried a little harder and she wanted to believe that Jace had stayed hidden until they got their hands on the keys and no one was in the house and that Wade had returned and found him. That's all she wanted to believe. She cried and she fell over on her side and lay there until she was done. And in the blackness it felt as if there was no difference between a minute and a thousand years.

She then began to hear things.

Whacks. Shouts.

Then the echoes of footsteps and voices reverberating through distant corridors. The voices of supplication. Maybe the voices of children mixed in with the resounding pleas. Jessie shifted across the floor with her bound hands outstretched, feeling her way and wanting to get a better listen. She ran her hands along the rough wall and felt the gunk of moss and mold and trailing water and she shrunk back at first touch but then held them there, wanting to find the door if there was one. She found the wooden beams joined together with bolted steel and found the small and barcovered opening and she held her ear to it. Believing she heard voices and thinking her mind was playing tricks with the sounds of the dark.

When the voices and movement died away there was the clang of steel slamming shut like some closing of the trap at the end of the world.

A long silence.

Then more footsteps moving through the corridors.

She moved her ear from the opening. Thunder roared in the world above ground. Jessie turned and rested her back against the door. She wondered if there was another door or if there was a window so she put her hands on the wall again and began to make her way around, feeling high and feeling low. Feeling the rainwater that was seeping through the earth and seeping between the cracks in the mortar. She made it to a corner and nothing. She continued on and felt a break in the wall, where the edges of broken brick and mortar were sharp and jagged. As if something had tried and failed to bust through. And then her foot hit something. She almost fell but caught her balance. And then she poked her foot out and bumped it again and smelled the smell and she knew she was both alone and not alone in the black and heartless void.

47

A DENSE AND UNTAMED LANDSCAPE drenched in darkness and rain. Wade drove along narrow roads and unmarked roads and roads covered in runnels of muddy water and he went down gravel roads and slick roads that ran along overgrown fields and disappeared into thick forests and he searched and searched to find the crossing that would seem familiar to him. He had no notion of direction and could only judge where he may be by the river that wound through the valley and formed the boundary between Louisiana and Mississippi. The riverwater ran high and strong and slapped against banks and bridges and the rain began to fall in sheets and sometimes it came in torrents. He sat parked and waiting when the storm was too much and he drank all the beer and smoked all the cigarettes. He told himself that he was close as he manipulated the landscape all through the night and then at dawn the rain began to relent and he knew that meant the eye of the storm was passing and then there would be the power of the backside of the hurricane. Fucking find it, he thought. Now. He had smoked everything and drunk everything save for one last drink in the bottom of the bottle of rye and he was saving that for courage.

48

HOLT LAY ON HIS BACK in three inches of water that was getting a little deeper all the time. He was bleeding and weak and a torch burned in the tunnel and the light filtered along the passageway and then disappeared into the dark. They had dropped him there and pulled the sack from his head and from what he could tell he had been left there to die and that's what he was doing. He listened to the drips of water that fell from the tunnel ceiling and he listened to the voices and clatters that sounded throughout the tunnels and his mind moved back and forth between the cold and painful reality and the dreamworld where he traversed each memory and misstep of the life he had lived. He imagined a world beyond that offered no reconciliation.

His nose and mouth were caked with blood and grime and his chest would not stop bleeding and he was wet with blood and dirty water. He lay with his eyes open and he thought of Elser's prophecy of the miracle child as the thunder boomed and the rain crashed and he wondered of miracles themselves. If there was such a thing. And then his mind turned to a sunfilled day when Jessie was pregnant. A day they spent driving with the windows down and then turning off into a field and moving over a hillside to be hidden from the road. They had unzipped and spread out a sleeping bag and lay on their backs. Her round belly and her placid eyes and the simplicity and beauty of a moment. They lay there until the sun began to fall toward the horizon and then Jessie had fallen asleep. Her hands across her stomach.

And while she slept he began to tell her about the scars because he knew that was the only way he could tell her. When she wasn't looking at him or listening to him. But he wanted to say it and he believed it may seep into her and that she would know and never have to ask him. He knew she wanted to know. And he loved her because she had never asked. So he told her about the man his mother wanted him to call dad. But I wouldn't do it, Holt said. His voice low and eyes to the sun and Jessie sleeping peacefully with his son growing inside of her. Because that wasn't who he was. He wasn't my dad and he wasn't even a man. Just wearing the skin of a man. And he never would leave me alone. That's all I wanted was for him to just leave me alone. I'd be sitting on the floor watching television and he would flick my ear and try to make me cry. His buddies there with him drinking beer and watching his little game. Laughing. Taunting me. When I wouldn't cry or even look at him he'd start twisting my earlobe and it hurt so goddamn bad but I would not fucking cry, not after that first time when he called me a pussy and they got a big kick out of that and whenever I said leave me alone it made it worse and that's the kind of man he was and there was no way I was going to call him dad. And I hated being anywhere with him even when she was there too and she knew I fucking hated him but she let him stay anyway. I didn't even see what happened to make the car run off the road. I just know he was driving and doing something he shouldn't have been doing when it flipped and then we were upside down. You could smell the gasoline right away and it was dripping and I was looking around and my mother wasn't there. She was thrown out. I was stuck and the gasoline dripped and he was there and he somehow got free and climbed out. I smelled gasoline and I smelled smoke and wherever it came from it made a trail and began to drip on my back. Drop after drop. I was stuck. Drop after drop. I watched him crawl out and crawl across the road. I called to him for help and he looked back at me and then he crawled off and then he was gone and the drip fell on my back and I heard the hiss and then I heard the snap. The spark. The flame. I wrestled and couldn't get loose and the gasoline kept dripping on my back it soaked my shirt and I heard the sirens coming and then I saw the flames rise out of the twisted metal and the sirens got closer and I got one leg free and got my arm and head out of the window and was waving to them and the fire engine raced toward me and I waved and the flames got bigger and I almost had my other leg free but my foot was caught and it was bleeding and I yanked and yanked and the men climbed out of the fire truck and were running toward me when there was a pop and the blaze spread and the back of my shirt caught fire and I couldn't get my foot loose and I was burning and I couldn't move or turn and then arms grabbed me and yanked and my foot sliced and they were beating me with coats or blankets or something and I don't remember anything else about it except for waking up facedown on a hospital bed, my whole body shaking and my back and my neck raw.

When he finished telling her he laid his hand next to hers on her stomach and then watched as the sun scorched the horizon and he waited for the blue to cool his thoughts of fire and hate. She slept into the gloam and when she woke he asked if she had dreamed of anything and she only stared back at him in the duskblue as if she had forgotten his name.

Now the water dripped around him. His scarred back against the cobblestones in the filthy water. And his thoughts returned to the life that was bleeding out of him and then he heard the voices of two men and the splashes of footsteps and then hands reached beneath his shoulders and lifted him to his feet. Pain ripped through his chest and he dropped right back down to his knees and both men lifted him again. And then in a deep and somber voice one of them said with impossible calm that it's time for you to see what you have decided to give your life for. It is time for you to witness.

He halfwalked while they dragged him along through the tunnel and he tried to gather himself and keep his mind through the shifting shadows. They turned a corner and the water grew deeper as the pathway declined, rising to their knees as they trudged along until they arrived at a narrow corridor. They stopped there and told him to stand up straight. Rise and behold.

Holt gathered all of his strength and he held upright. He looked at the men as if suddenly realizing they were there and they were as faceless as lurkers in a sordid dream. He then stared down the corridor. A set of stone steps rose from the water and led to an elevated door and the keys rested in the lock of the bulky door. A torch flamed above the door and glowed like the burning sun on the fading day of the hillside confession he had made to the sleeping Jessie and it took him back to the sunlight of promise and a sky filled with hope and with that burning sun in his mind he reached down and snatched the knife from the sheath on the man's belt and he slashed one throat and was reaching to slash another when a hard fist landed right between his eyes. He buckled and dropped the knife into the water and the man pounced on Holt, his hands around his throat and holding him beneath the kneehigh water with all of his weight and Holt splashed and grabbed and slapped at the man's arms and all was going blurry as the last of the air was being choked away and that's when his hand found the blade beneath the water and with whatever strength he had left he shoved the knife into the man's stomach and twisted and the man screamed in agony and turned loose of Holt's throat. Holt came up from the water choking but shoving the knife deeper and the blood spilled into the rising water. Holt drove the knife and now he pushed the man underneath the water and held him below by his hair and in a moment the fight was gone from him. Holt pulled out the blade. Fell back down into the water with a great exhaustion. His own wounds carrying him to the end. His own strength spent. He dropped the knife and let it sink and he raised his dying eyes toward the door at the end of the corridor.

And then he watched as his spirit separated from his own body. It was not in the form of his adultself but instead it was in the form of a boy. A scarless and curious boy. He slumped down into the flooding corridor, resting on his elbows with his chin just above the water as he watched the shifting figure of his boyhood move to the end of the corridor and settle on the stone steps. Holt raised his hand from the water and pointed a limp finger at the burning torch and then he spoke in the silent language of the dead.

Go and see. She is there. I know she is there.

49

JESSIE HEARD THE MAN'S SCREAM reverberate through the underground. And it was then she decided that she would rather die being able to see than die in the dark. She worked the knot on the drawstring until it loosened and came free and she pulled the sack from her head. Heavy breaths of relief as her eyes adjusted and the dull torchlight of the tunnels gave the slightest dimension of shadow. She then chewed and gnawed at the layers of duct tape wrapping her wrists until she was able to make a split and she caught the tear between her teeth and worked and worked until she could separate her hands. She tore the layers away and threw them into the dark corner of her chamber which she wouldn't look into because that's where the body lay. She stood at the door and looked out of the opening, unaware if it was day or night or if it was tomorrow or if there was no goddamn tomorrow in this place. Only water death thunder.

There was no keyhole for the door though so she put her arm through the opening and rose to her tiptoes and tried to reach down and feel the plank or strip of iron or whatever it might be that held the door shut but she could not reach it. She put her face against the iron bars of the opening and looked back and forth. Along the passageway the water ran along the cobblestones in silvered ripples and black smoke from the torches held against the arched ceiling. She rubbed her eyes as if that may deliver a greater light or clarity to the scene but nothing changed. She turned and slumped with her back against the door. A strange sense of agedness came over her, believing if she did ever escape and return to Jace that he would be a grown man and that the streets and buildings she knew would be abandoned and the skies would be a swirl of smoke and storm and there would be tombstones for the faces she could remember.

50

WHAT WADE REMEMBERED MOST WAS the feeling of being at the end of the road. The nearness of oblivion. All night and through daybreak everything looked the same and felt the same but now he was at a crossing and the truck tires sat on the last of the asphalt and to the right and to the left and straight ahead were only the rainsplashed and unpaved roads of nowhere. He put his trust into the memory of eighteen years ago and turned left.

The wind blew in violent circles inside the eye of the storm and the untamed wood swayed in the great swirl. The road shrunk down just as Wade recalled and the limbs and brush batted against the truck like a violent mob. When he came to the wetlands the water had risen above the road and he shifted the truck into low gear and kept on, the wind pushing the truck and pushing the water and the cypress bending and bowing and he leaned on the steering wheel mumbling in prayers of continuation. He kept mumbling and the wind whipped and the truck worked hard through it all until he finally saw the rise in the road and he began to ascend from the blackwater.

The truck climbed the hill slowly. Wade stopped when he reached the crest and looked over the edge. The wild had grown up the other side and now nearly reached the hilltop and he shifted into park. No way to go any further.

He reached across the bench seat and he picked up the flashlight and the pistol. And then he grabbed the bottle of rye and he turned it up and finished it. He tossed the empty bottle and got out of the truck.

He began, moving down the slope and stepping through vine and brush. Trying to move straight ahead and trying to imagine it all in the headlights of the past and trying to convince himself the whole thing hadn't been some drunken and misremembered vision. He pushed forward and down, the ground covered in rainsodden leaves and fallen limbs and he kept on straight until he noticed the clearing. He moved faster then, believing it was all there. He moved into the clearing and the pathway remained and stretched toward the walls.

He ran with his arms out in front and defending against the wayward limbs that slapped in the gusts and he came to the end of the path and stood there looking at the gate. Extended from the top of the gate was a wroughtiron cross that was unbothered by the wind.

The walls were smothered with decades of moss and vine and the gate was made of iron bars as thick as arms. Honeysuckle twisted through the bars and rainclung spiderwebs stretched through the honeysuckle and a snake wrapped itself around the bottom bar of the gate and stared at the intruder with bottomless eyes. The wall extended in both directions, camouflaged by a dense and sunless wood where the trees stood together through the storms like a gathered militia. The leaves no longer knew the seasons here and held to limbs in shades of yellow and red and green.

Wade stepped to the gate. He reached through the vines and found a handle. It was rusted and stubborn but it turned and then he pushed the gate against the clutches of vine and he made enough room to squeeze through. The snake slithered down from the iron bar and moved across Wade's foot as he entered into the secreted world and he leapt and held the pistol on it as it flicked its tongue and disappeared into brush.

He hurried on. Beyond the gate a pathway moved in slack curves. The terrain was sloppy and sunken and in stretches the pathway was swallowed by water. He ran and splashed and tripped in the giving earth and fell and got up again and kept on. And then he began to see the marks of man.

Boats that offered deeper passage into the swamps were tied to the trunks of trees with gnarly lengths of rope. And the landscape became littered. Clothes and shoes were strewn on the ground and thrown into the trees. Cages made for large animals were bunched in a messy stack. Lengths of barbed wire stretched between limbs where wooden crosses and shotguns and arms and legs of mannequins hung from the barbed wire by lengths of chain and knocked together in the wind. Wade walked carefully, ducking the barbed wire. Watching the path ahead for something he should not step into and then when he was clear of the strips of barbed wire, he looked up. Hanged corpses swung from tree limbs in various stages of decay. Morbid and noiseless windchimes of the deep wood. He swallowed hard and then spit and he could not help but search for his daughter swinging in the trees but she was not there. He then bent over and vomited.

He wiped his mouth and kept on and then the woods opened and there was sky. The hurricane sky and the rush of the wind and the slategray to the south that promised that more was on its way. On the other side of the opening he saw the fortress built into a hillside, a rivervein running the length of the hillside. Behind the fortress a blackdirt road wound up the incline and disappeared into the woods and a swinging bridge stretched across the rivervein and reached to the fortress, hanging just above the strong and shifting current. Cannons poked out from concrete eyes and the bricks had crumbled and fallen away like bad teeth but the kudzu crawled and blanketed the hillside and draped the fortress as if to protect it from collapse. Arched entries and exits surrounded the base of the fortress and sloped immediately to belowground caverns where light disappeared and the water had begun to rise above the bank and bleed over into the caverns.

Wade ran across the clearing and he tucked the pistol and flashlight into his beltline and grabbed hold of the ropes of the swinging bridge. Fighting the wind and ignoring the current below and avoiding the missing slats as he made it across and to the Bottom where he ducked into the cover of the caverns. He paused and listened and heard only the natural world. He wiped the water from his face and eyes. Tried to believe he was somewhere he should have been. And then he flicked on the flashlight and shined it into the shrouded passageway and he slipped into the darkness.

51

JESSIE WAS LEANED AGAINST THE door trying to keep her mind when the gunshot rang and energized her senses. Then a litter of gunfire and shouting tore through the underground and she turned and looked out and she screamed for Holt in the midst of the commotion and then just as soon as it all began, it was over. She held the bars and waited for something more. She heard random voices and movement and the trickle of water between the cracks. She moved to where she had found the crumbling space in the wall and she knelt and found a piece of brick the size of a baseball and she moved back to the door and listened again.

Then voices and the movement of shadows down the passageway. Footsteps splashing through the water. She moved into the shadowy depths of the holding and she slipped the sack back over her head and she lay down next to the corpse. She crossed her hands as if bound and she clutched the brick in her right hand. The splashing came closer and then it stopped when it reached her. The thud of the brace being removed from the door. The footsteps moving inside. Pausing and looking for her and then seeing her next to the body.

'Not yet,' the voice said. Her world dark inside the sack but feeling him closer and feeling the water splash on her back when he stepped to her. The hands reached down and grabbed her by the shoulders and turned her over and she rose and swung blind and the brick landed against a forehead and she jerked the sack from her head. He had fallen on his rear end and in the moment of daze she swung and hit him again and he fell back and she pounced and bashed the brick against his head until she heard the crack and then she dropped the brick and fell back on the concrete. Her hand shook and was covered in blood and she washed it off in the water she sat in. When she went to get up she was trembling and lightheaded and she held the wall and tried to gather herself. She slowed her breathing. Slowed the tremble. Then she dragged the man to the other side of the holding where he lay unconscious with the dead. She closed and braced the door and then she stepped lightly, trying not to splash as she held the brick and moved through the passageway.

52

WADE STAYED CROUCHED AND CLOSE to the wall as he moved through the arched passageways, torchlit and filling with water. He heard the gunshot and then the rattle of gunfire and he shrunk away from any light as he clutched the pistol and waited for the uproar to come charging his way. But it died down and he stood very still and waited on the silence before he moved again. He moved with the pistol raised and ready and used the flashlight along the darker passages and it was true. There were people here and they were bad people and this was a bad place but it meant that she could be here.

When he found her she was in the corridor. The torch burning above the door. The water up to her waist. He recognized the solitary nature of her silhouette. He shined the flashlight on her and she had her hands on Holt's floating body. She had pulled up his shirt and was touching the scars on his back.

'Jessie,' Wade said.

She raised her head in astonishment and looked toward the beam. Wade lowered the light from her face and stepped into the corridor, the water higher and higher as the corridor descended and she held Holt with one hand and she reached out for Wade with the other and he took it. Wade saw the scars and knew.

'Are you hurt?' he said.

'No.'

'We have to go.'

'I don't want to leave him.'

'I know you don't and I don't want you to but we have to.'

'No.'

'I found Jace. He's safe. He's waiting for you.'

She turned her eyes to Wade. Something seemed to fall from her and then her expression gathered weight as she processed the chaos surrounding them. She then turned Holt over in the water where she could see his face. There were voices and splashing and Wade said we have to get the hell out of here. Jessie wiped the hair away from Holt's eyes and then she nodded to Wade.

The splashing came closer and there was nothing to do but wait and see. Wade raised the pistol and held it aimed at the opening of the corridor. The torchlight glowed brighter and the shadows grew more distinct and there was hard coughing and choking and then they appeared. The wiry figure of Elser and the tall man. She held a torch and his arm was draped around her neck and he was limplegged and shot up and coughing blood. She looked at them down the corridor and the tall man dropped from her. He fell to his knees and then more coughing and gagging and then his air was gone and he collapsed face first into the water.

'Don't move,' Wade said.

She stepped into the corridor as if she didn't hear him and she was in another place and time. Her eyes drawn to the door and the burning torch above it. As she crept toward them the corridor became illuminated in firelight and she recognized the keys in the lock. Wade warned her again and she ignored him again and the water rose on her small frame as she seemed to be drifting now. Her eyes attached to the door as she moved right past them, the pistol an arm's length from her head but she was not aware or did not care.

'I am here,' Elser said as she floated toward the end of the corridor. 'For you. For me.'

Wade took Jessie by the arm and tried to head them out but Jessie would not move.

'Let go,' she said.

He pulled again. She jerked her arm free and followed after Elser.

'What the hell are you doing?'

'I… I want to see.'

He grabbed her again but she jerked away again.

'I said let go of me,' she said. Her eyes hard on Wade and then shifting into some kind of placation. 'I have to know.'

Elser made it to the end of the corridor and she climbed the steps and rose from the water as if in baptismal ascension. Jessie trailed Elser in the waisthigh water. Mesmerized. Wade followed Jessie and called to her to stop but she was not listening. When Elser reached the top of the steps she held the torch to the keys and she looked back at Jessie and Wade with a girlish smile, her eyes dancing in the light. And then she faced the door and she turned the key. The metal shift of the lock moving and then she pushed the door and it opened with an ancient groan. Jessie began to hurry through the water and Wade called out once more and she was almost to the steps when he caught her by the back of her shirt. Jessie paused when he pulled and they both looked up to where Elser stood in the open door with the look of the amazed. She called out her own name into the darkness. Elser. Elser. I am here. She then turned her torchlit eyes back to them in some otherworld satisfaction just as two filthy arms reached out from the dark behind the door and yanked her inside.

Jessie shrieked and then shrieked louder as she turned to Wade and they grabbed hands and ran. Slowlegged running through the water of the corridor and then racing through the caverns and he led them the way he had come with the pistol at the ready and neither of them looking back to see what may be behind them and they made turns and heard gunshots and screams and they kept running until they saw the faint light of day at the end of the passageway and they kept running until they were out of the Bottom and helping one another across the tattered bridge that now skipped in the rising current and they kept running past the hanged corpses and the barbed wire and the boats and they began to climb the slope, slipping and falling in the rain and wind and helping one another and then seeing the truck. Their arms and faces slashed from the limbs and brush as they made it up the incline and into the truck and from what they could see through the rainstreaked windshield there was no one behind them.

53

THERE WAS NOTHING TO DO but wait out the remaining hours of hurricane. When they made it back into the truck cab Wade asked Jessie again if she was hurt in any way. Her face was bruised and she had a cut on her chin and her hair was tangled but she shook her head and said she was okay. She asked him about Jace and he explained that he had found him hiding in the closet and then he had left him with Alvin and Melissa and he was safe as long as Alvin's red-neck hurricane defense system held the mobile home in place. Wade found a rag in the glovebox and they used it to wipe their faces and necks and he cranked the truck and turned on the heat, trying to defend against the chill of their wet clothes.

He said he was sorry about Holt and she made no answer and then they sat in silence for a long while, the sky growing dark and the back end of the storm beating down and the heavy woods bending. The truck rocked in the gusts and a falling limb smacked against the hood. Wade turned off the engine and Jessie slumped against the door in exhaustion, moved to the edge of tears now but she sucked the rising emotions back down. Finally she slept.

Wade held the pistol and watched the storm and watched the landscape out before them for anyone or anything that might be coming in their direction. Jessie shifted in her sleep and sometimes said something and sometimes raised her hand and waved it as if fending away an enemy but her eyes stayed closed and she would settle and continue to sleep. Whenever she moved or spoke some fragment in her dreamworld he would look at her and all he could see was the child he left alone.

When Jessie finally woke hours later he began talking about her mother. He explained he had known Rebecca since seventh grade and he had liked her and then loved her all through high school and it took him forever to find the courage to ask her on a date and when he finally found his nerve, she said no. And she said no about a dozen more times before she finally said yes and he had always made fun of her for being so easy when years later she said yes to his marriage proposal on the first try. He told Jessie about the way she wore her hair and how she walked and the way she rolled her eyes at dumb jokes. He told her that her favorite thing about summer was the lightning bugs dancing in the woods and her favorite thing about winter was the silvery brush of jack frost. He told her that Rebecca took good photographs and could hold her liquor and that she had a scar on her knee from where she skinned it badly as a child. He went on and on and when he finally stopped, Jessie shifted in the seat and turned toward him and leaned forward a little. The pose of inquiry. She began to ask the questions she always had about her mother. And he answered them.

54

MELISSA WAS HOLDING JACE AND looking out of the window. The labored hum of a running generator outside. The worst of it all gone and the mobile home still standing. A drip of water from the ceiling made a damp spot in the carpet next to where Melissa stood as she and the boy looked out into the dark and watched the lightning flash in the distant sky. Another storm moving away.

The headlights appeared in the distance, two white beacons rifling through the night. The truck made its way along the road and then pulled onto the property and she called Alvin to come over here. He was sitting around the coffee table with his pigtailed daughters and playing cards by lamplight and he laid his cards down and warned them not to cheat and he joined her at the window. They watched as the truck shifted between the vehicles and the junk. It rolled right up to the steps of the deck and the headlights cut off and the engine cut off. A long and motionless moment followed and Melissa slipped her hand into Alvin's hand as they waited. Jace raised his small finger and pointed out into the dark. And then the truck doors opened and closed and two slumped silhouettes moved through the rain and up the stairs and there was a knock on the door.

EPILOGUE

THE FLATBED TRUCK HAD BEEN sitting on the crop road and watching the house for ten minutes. A half-dozen deer wandered through the kneehigh grass surrounding the house and the old car that sat parked by the front steps. The deer paused to regard the blue smoke coming from the tailpipe of the chugging diesel engine and then continued on with their noses down and whitetails up. The couple in the flatbed passed a quart of beer back and forth.

'See. There ain't nobody here. Just like I told you,' the man said.

'Don't look like it,' she answered.

'Was the same yesterday and the day before.'

'Just hold on another minute.'

Their booty was strapped across the back of the flatbed, a sloppy pile of refrigerators and lawnmowers and kitchen stoves. A clutter of anything they thought may be of value at the junkyard or by the side of the road where they sat in lawnchairs with a sign that read MAKE OFFER. The woman wore a bandana tied around her head to keep her frizzy hair out of her face and she tapped her finger on her knee as she watched and waited.

'I'm telling you,' he said. The man's hands rested on the steering wheel and they were rough and callused. Spotted with age. Half of his pinky finger was missing from a job at the mill way back when there were jobs at the mill. She swigged from the quart and handed it to him.

'All right,' she said. 'Go on.'

He shifted into drive and the flatbed moved toward the house. On each side of the crop road the cornstalks lay in crumbled heaps but for the random stalk that held erect in a stubborn refusal of fate. The deer sprang away in beautiful leaps as the truck pulled across the yard, the high grass brushing the chassis beneath. The man parked behind the hatchback and killed the engine and the land fell silent. They sat there a moment in the peace of wild things and then they got out.

The hatchback rested on flat tires and was covered in grime and bits of what remained of gunshot glass hung in the rims of the windows. The man ran his finger across the top of the car and then he looked inside. Glass lay scattered across the seats and floorboards. A pungent smell met him as he leaned his head in and he groaned and held his nose. He saw the key was in the ignition and he pulled back from the window and let out a big breath and he slapped his hand on the hood.

'It might only need a battery,' he said.

'You say that every time we find a car.'

'Well. It might.'

'Has that ever worked?'

'No but that don't mean it won't.'

'Jesus Lord,' she said.

'No sense in arguing about it.'

'I ain't talking about that. Jesus Lord.'

'What?'

She was on the other side of the car and she pointed to the ground. He walked around the hatchback and looked to where she motioned to the skeleton. The grass had grown between its bones and it appeared to be facedown. The clothes were pecked and torn by the hooked beaks of vultures. A gun lay next to the fingers.

'I told you nobody was here,' the man said. 'Not for a long time it don't seem like.'

'Somebody should bury him.'

'Don't look at me.'

He reached and took her by the arm and pulled her along. They moved around the hatchback and toward the porch steps, pausing to give the exterior a onceover. Shingles and roofing paper had been ripped away by the wind and left exposed sheathing that was rotted and discolored. There was a gunshot through the window and gunshots splintered the woodframe around the door and a porch post. A coffee cup sat next to a rocking chair. The door was open.

'I don't feel good about this place,' she said.

'We've seen stuff like this.'

'I know. But I ain't never felt this way about any of them.'

'How's it feel then?'

'Like something is living here.'

'There ain't nothing here.'

'I know it,' she snapped. 'I said it feels like it.'

The man was not deterred and he moved up the steps. She followed him and they walked inside. The furniture was toppled and there were more gunshots in the walls. The hardwood floor was warped and littered with animal droppings and the intruding wind had whipped trash and leaves around the room. Some type of nest had been made in the corner of the hearth. The ceiling was dripping and waterstained and its yellowbrown pattern stretched out like some expanding map of a frightening new world.

'How come you'd shoot a television?' the man said and he nodded at the wounded screen.

They stepped through the clutter. The kitchen table was on its side and pocked with buckshot and an empty bottle of whiskey sat on the counter with one murky drink left that was covered in a thick mold. A brown trail crossed the linoleum floor and reached to the hardwood and they both knew it was old blood. The man moved to the microwave and he opened and closed the door and then he stepped to the kitchen sink. He looked out of the window above the sink and saw the shed in the back of the house. A pine tree lay across the damaged roof and the doors of the shed were open and he saw the nose of the riding lawnmower.

'There's a good payday,' he said.

'What?'

'Out back. Shed full of stuff. All of this shit in here is too old and moldy. I wouldn't open that refrigerator if I was you.'

He moved through the kitchen and opened up the back door and walked out. Through the window she saw him cross the yard toward the shed. She put her hands on her hips and let out a sigh. Then she looked toward the hallway. I know nobody is here, she told herself. I know nobody is here. She rubbed her hands together as if to warm herself to the assurance that she was alone. Then she stepped into the shadows.

She went into the first bedroom and the woman could tell it was the bedroom of a girl. The posters of teenage dreams and the purple pillowcases and pinkstriped blanket wadded on the floor. The emptied jewelry box beside the blanket. The drawers had been pulled from the dresser and thrown on the floor and the woman knelt and picked through, thinking there may be a ring or a watch or something of value that had been missed by whoever did all of this but instead she found a crayon drawing of a mother and child. She picked it up and the paper was soft and weathered. She studied the faded colors of the sun and the joined hands and the dog in the yard. Outside the man rattled around in the shed and then he called out something to her. She stood and moved to the window and he was walking across the yard with a toolbox. He stopped when he came to the HVAC unit and she leaned against the wall and watched as he went to work disconnecting it. She then folded the drawing and stuck it in her pocket and she left the girl's bedroom and crossed the hall into the other room.

The woodpanel wall was bowed and the ceiling sagged but the photographs remained on the wall. She stepped across the overturned mattress and straddled the bedframe as she looked at the faces. The man and the woman and the little girl. Though she noticed the three of them were not together in any of the frames. And then she admired the school photographs of the girl, watching her grow from first grade and into middle school and realizing that the older she got the less she smiled.

It gets rough, the woman thought.

She touched her finger to the forced grin of adolescence. The recognition of something gone away. Then she touched the damp and misshapen wall and she listened to the racket of plunder outside. And as she stared into the eyes of the girl she marveled at the strength it takes to salvage this world.

ACKNOWLEDGMENTS

Many thanks to Ellen Levine, Josh Kendall, Sabrina Callahan, Yuli Masinovsky, Jason Richman, and the teams at Little, Brown and Trident Media Group. Many more thanks to Sabrea, Presley, and Brooklyn.